Trouble Comes To Palmer Lake
The Unwelcome Stranger

Bob Ensley & Gordon Endicott

Outskirts Press, Inc.
Denver, Colorado

This is a work of fiction. The events and characters described herein are imaginary and are not intended to refer to specific places or living persons. The opinions expressed in this manuscript are solely the opinions of the author and do not represent the opinions or thoughts of the publisher. The author has represented and warranted full ownership and/or legal right to publish all the materials in this book.

Trouble Comes To Palmer Lake
The Unwelcome Stranger
All Rights Reserved.
Copyright © 2010 Bob Ensley & Gordon Endicott
v2.0

Cover Photo © 2010 JupiterImages Corporation. All rights reserved - used with permission.

This book may not be reproduced, transmitted, or stored in whole or in part by any means, including graphic, electronic, or mechanical without the express written consent of the publisher except in the case of brief quotations embodied in critical articles and reviews.

Outskirts Press, Inc.
http://www.outskirtspress.com

ISBN: 978-1-4327-6470-8

Outskirts Press and the "OP" logo are trademarks belonging to Outskirts Press, Inc.

PRINTED IN THE UNITED STATES OF AMERICA

Chapter One

"Barbershop, this is Travis."
"Is it really you?"
"Now what do you think?"
"If I knew the answer already, would I be asking?"
"Corky, you smart-aleck. Where are you?"
"What do you mean, where am I?"
"Did you forget already? Tonight's the get together at the barbershop!"
"Oh, that's right! I've been so busy today fixing toilets, I forgot."
"You and your thrones. Don't you ever wonder what people think of you?"
"Not really. I know they can't wait to sit on their properly working best friend again, so it all evens out with a good flush."
"Just get over here. I need to talk to you about something that's really bugging me!"

"Like what?"

"Like, I'll tell you when you get here. And Corky, remember, we're having story telling after checkers."

"What's tonight's subject again?"

"We're each telling how we wound up here in Palmer Lake."

"Who all's coming, anyhow?"

"Some of my regular customers, plus a couple of their relatives from out of state."

"The relatives wouldn't happen to be good looking women, would they?"

"No such luck, Corky."

"Well, I guess I better go get cleaned up."

"Try using soap this time."

"Very funny."

"Corky, I've got to go. Toot just showed up. I'll see you when you get here."

Toot is one of the regulars at Travis's barbershop. He hangs around playing checkers with Travis on a daily basis.

"Hey, Toot, I see you got all dressed up for the get-together."

"I've got my special shirt on, Travis."

"I see it still has that big stain on the sleeve."

"Been there for as long as I can remember, Travis."

"And how long is that?"

"I can't remember."

Toot is older than Travis's vintage guitar

collection. I don't think anybody knows his real age. But that doesn't matter. He's one of the good guys here in town. With Toot being at the barbershop tonight, Travis made sure the fan was blowing on a towel soaked in aftershave.

"Well, look there, Toot, the Birdman has arrived."

"Travis, you've already started sipping your bourbon. Couldn't wait for the rest of us?"

"I've never waited, Birdman. That's how I built my reputation with the ladies."

"Don't start, Travis. The ladies are the reason you came to Palmer Lake, to hide out!"

"There was only one gal I had to get away from, and I certainly wouldn't call her a lady!"

"I've heard that her face would have frightened my parrots into the next county."

"Okay, Birdie, enough is enough."

The Birdman is another member of our old timers fraternity. He surrounds himself with dozens of birds at home, all flying around loose, dropping on everything, including him.

By six-thirty, everybody had shown up, except me. The other regulars included Fletch, Dawson, Reed and Lyle. Dawson brought his uncle Clay and his dad Hank, who were the relatives vacationing here in Palmer Lake.

When I finally arrived, the guys were about to start their first round of checkers. It took me more time to clean off the grime than I'd planned. Better late than filthy, I always say.

"Gentlemen, welcome our local handyman. If your wife has plumbing problems, just call Corky!"

"Evening fellows, sorry I'm late. Travis's sister called just as I was getting ready to leave. Seems she's been eating red snapper, and plugged up her crapper!"

"Thanks, Corky. I'll be sure to have her put you in the will."

The evening's checkers games were played with plenty of four-letter words, mostly from Birdman. Hank took the evening's trophy, which was a six-pack of beer that a customer had left Travis as a tip.

It was about time for the story telling to begin, so we all took turns visiting the head, then pulled the chairs into a circle and drew numbers out of Toot's old baseball cap to see who would go first. Being the host of this gathering, Travis wasn't allowed to pick a number. First up was Birdman.

"Okay, no interruptions while I'm telling my story, or I'll have some of my birds spend the night at your house!

"Now, to begin with, I moved to Palmer Lake about twelve years ago, after being offered the head of security position at Palmer Industries. I was single, so there wasn't any reason not to come give it a try. I liked what I saw and thought the clean air would be good for raising my birds."

TROUBLE COMES TO PALMER LAKE

"I want you guys to notice the very high, very tight, Marine Corps style of haircut that the Birdman wears. That's my work you're seeing."

"Travis, next you'll be telling them about my operation, and why I walk with a limp! I thought it was my turn to tell my own story! As you guys will see, once Travis gets started, there's no stopping him."

"Birdman, are you still fondling turkeys on Thanksgiving? The only reason they let you is because they admire your haircut!"

"You see what I mean? I hope you guys are prepared for this. These interruptions will go on all night. I'm done!"

"Which one of you has number two? Was it you, Toot?"

"Yep. Let me take off my cap so I look more presentable. I'm going to sit in the captain's chair and be nice to my backside.

"Well, first off, my real name isn't Toot. It's Bailey Ficklin. My friends just call me Toot. I don't remember how that name ever got started, but it suits me fine. A man needs a good nickname to get through the hard times, and I've seen plenty.

"I first visited Palmer Lake when I was a young boy. My folks used to rent a cabin every summer so we could go swimming and row a boat. I kept up the family tradition by moving here, back when I had me a wife.

"One day she ran off with my brother, and I

haven't seen either of them since. It was shortly after that I came down with intestinal problems the doctors still haven't put a name to. Been with me ever since."

"Gentlemen, if you would like to hear more of Toot's story, you'll have to take him outside. I'm afraid he's going to scorch the upholstery on my barber chair. Who's up next with number three?"

Next came Lyle, followed by Dawson, Reed and Fletch. They all had similar tales to tell about moving to Palmer Lake, and they were as boring as a Sunday afternoon visit to the retirement home. I felt sorry for Clay and Hank. I think they would have gotten up and walked out, had they each drank a few more beers.

Everyone had taken a turn, except Travis and me.

"Okay, Corky, it's your turn to tell these guys where the bear dumped in the buckwheat."

"Thanks, Travis. Hey guys, I'm Corky Perkins, the local handyman. I used to live north of here about sixty miles in a small town called Happy Valley, where I worked in an auto parts store and played in a country western band on the weekends.

"One Saturday night, while playing at the Cow Pie Tavern, a good-looking gal named Lydia kept brushing up against me when she and her boyfriend Fred were on the dance floor. During our break, Fred went outside to have a smoke and Lydia invited me to visit her at their table.

TROUBLE COMES TO PALMER LAKE

"At the end of the night, as I was loading my gear into my truck, here came Lydia, all by herself. Maybe it was her perfume, I don't know, but five minutes later, the two of us were heading out of town in her car to an all night restaurant for coffee and donuts. All I could think about was Fred coming after me with his welding torch when he found out that Lydia and I had snuck out together.

"Lydia and Fred were a long-time couple that everyone in town knew. Besides being a welder, Fred was also considered the local strong man. He once lifted a car up by its bumper, freeing town mechanic Greasy Leo, after the floor jack collapsed.

"On my next day off, I had plans to go to the laundromat and visit the western wear store for a new cowboy shirt. I headed out the front door of my house, and to my surprise, there in the driveway sat Lydia. She asked me to come to her apartment after I was done with my errands.

"I know what you guys are thinking - why not just go for it, right? Well, I showed up at her apartment at around three o'clock and when the door opened, there stood some guy. I asked if I was at Lydia's apartment, and he invited me in. I was half expecting Fred to jump out of the closet, but instead, out came Lydia from the bathroom, wrapped in a towel! At that point, I made up something about how I hadn't finished doing my laundry, and I couldn't stay.

"I headed home, packed up my belongings, left

my roommates a note, and hit the road. I was sure that Fred would hear from town folk that I had been involved in a three-way with his girlfriend and some guy named Tim!

"I kept driving till I ran out of gas, here in Palmer Lake. I rented a room at the Legend Motel and the next day I found a job at the local hardware store.

"A couple weeks later, a store customer happened to ask if we knew of someone who could repair a toilet. I raised my hand, and the rest is history."

"Okay, gents, Corky ran a little long with his sad, boohoo tale about Lydia. If it had been me, I'd have taken her to the Travis Tower Amusement Park and let her ride all night! Not to some lousy restaurant for donuts."

"Travis, you think you're really something when it comes to your manhood. Rumor around here has it that my youngest parrot has a bigger pecker than you!"

"Gentlemen, you have just heard it straight from the Birdman's mouth. He keeps his gaggle of birds around so he can stare at peckers all day!"

"I only speak the truth, Travis."

"Birdman, at least mine doesn't have feathers on it!"

"Travis, are you going to tell your story, or are you and Birdman going to keep spewing hot air? If I have to listen to any more of it, I'm going to

TROUBLE COMES TO PALMER LAKE

need another round of antacids!"

"Toot, since when did you become my keeper?"

"Just tell your story, Travis. But give me a minute before you start. I feel another trip to the indoor outhouse coming on."

While Toot was making his way to the back of the shop, he let one rip. The others all started laughing. The vacationers said they hadn't ever had this much fun, and couldn't wait to hear more.

Travis kept trying to pull me aside so he could tell me what was bugging him, but the other guys kept butting in.

We wound up waiting a lot longer than a minute for Toot, but finally, it was Travis's turn. He decided to sit in the barber chair as well, since it was a lot more comfortable.

"Once upon a time…"

"Oh, screw that, Travis. This isn't a fairy tale!"

"Thanks, Birdman. I can always count on your mouth!"

"That's what Rosie told the butcher!"

"Gentlemen, my name is Travis O'Riley, and I'm the local barber here in Palmer Lake. I once was a big city dweller, though, and I liked the bright lights and the fast pace.

"I met a gal who became the love of my life, and we wound up getting married. I figured the honeymoon would last forever, but World War Three broke out, and the marriage ended abruptly.

After that, I quit my job and sold everything I owned, except my van and my guitar.

"Before getting married, I had spent time playing music in taverns, for drinks, tips, and women. So, I decided to try it again. I hooked up with a musician named Paul, and we did pretty well together on stage.

"Then, one evening when I went to pick him up for our gig, he was nowhere to be found. To this day, I've never heard from the guy!

"After that, I put away my guitar and hit the road. My travels took me to many different cities and towns. I held a variety of jobs during those years, such as washing dishes, and working in lumber and steel mills. But my favorite job was working at a little shop that sold accessories for lovers. I also kept my hand in barbering, when I could find a shop in need of my services.

"Being on the road wore me down, and I felt like I needed to find a place to roost. I happened to stop in Palmer Lake one day, and something seemed to grab me by the collar and whisper, 'Welcome home, Travis.'

"While driving around town, I discovered this barbershop. Back then, it was owned by an old man named Charlie Potts. I stopped in to have a look, and wound up talking Charlie into giving me a try. After a week or so, he offered me a job.

"Then, a couple months later, old Charlie passed away, and that's when I worked out a deal with his widow to buy the place."

"What kind of a deal was it, Travis?"

"Stuff it, Birdie."

"During my first year here, I spent several evenings at Pop's Saloon, with my guitar. The local stardom was just what I needed to make me feel good again. Unfortunately, that all came to an end when Pop decided to retire and close down.

"A few months later, a lady by the name of Bertha Babber arrived in town and bought the old Pop's Saloon place. She spent a few months remodeling it, and then opened it back up as Bertha's Teardrop Lounge.

"Bertha is a large woman, not what you would call fat, rather voluptuous, actually. But something about her seemed rather scary.

"One afternoon she stopped in the barbershop looking for me, because several of the locals had been requesting my music. She demanded that I start playing again that night! I knew better than to say no to Bertha!"

"You ever take her to the Travis Tower Amusement Park?"

"Birdman, stick a sock in it."

"Stick a what in where, Travis?"

"Toot, don't pay any attention. Birdman's been away from his gaggle too long and now he's going flocking crazy."

"Did you go a few rounds with Bertha or not, Travis?"

"The only rounds I've had with Bertha are the ones we drank together at the lounge. Now, clean up your mouth, Dirty Birdie!

"So, boys, that's my story and I'm sticking to it. I play music at Bertha's from time to time with my good friend Corky. Together, we make the ladies crawl all over us. Isn't that right, Corky?"

"What he says is true, gentlemen. A gal even pulled me off stage one night and dragged me into the women's room. I managed to escape as she was trying to strip off her skin tight, double-extra-large jeans. I got a standing ovation for that one, and Travis never missed a beat."

"Well, boys, it's getting late and some of us real men have to get up early for work. Hope you all enjoyed yourselves, and thanks for showing up. And remember, my name is Travis O'Riley, and I own this place. Now get the hell out of here!"

Chapter Two

Travis had been trying all evening to talk to me about whatever was bugging him, and now that the others were gone, he finally got his chance.

"Corky, this might sound pretty strange, but it's been driving me nuts all day!"

"Well, Travis, let it out!"

"Today when I opened up, there wasn't much happening other than the old town dog making his morning visit to the corner garbage can. It was about an hour before I got my first customer.

"The guy was a stranger, and I could tell by his manner of dress he was well healed. He wore the biggest gold ring I've ever seen. The way he carried himself seemed a bit unnerving, though, and when I introduced myself, his reply was ice cold."

"What did you expect him to say?"

"Corky, people who come in here, even the occasional stranger, like to shoot the bull. But not this guy. He was anything but friendly."

"Travis, some people are like that. It reminds me of old what's-his-name, with the glass eye, that lives over on Hunkins Street."

"You must be talking about Willis Miles."

"That's the guy! When I went to his place to repair a shower door, all he wanted to know was, how much? He laid the money on the kitchen table, and I never saw him after that. I don't know where he went, but I know he didn't leave, because my truck was blocking his car in."

"Well, Corky, there's more to my story than the guy just being unfriendly. When he went over to hang up his jacket on the coat rack, I spotted a shoulder holster. He was packing!"

"Like, he's a cop?"

"Trust me, Corky, this guy's no cop."

"What did you do?"

"I just kept talking while I cut his hair. He must have dropped his guard a bit after seeing the quality of the haircut, because I asked him where he was from and he said Chicago. Then he asked me if I knew where he could find some gal by the name of Sherry Winter."

"Sherry Winter? Who's that?"

"I don't know. I've never heard of her."

"Well, Travis, you can't take this personal. Maybe his old lady took off with his brother, too."

"That could be. But get this - I finished him up and he tipped me ten dollars! Nobody has ever tipped me ten bucks!"

"I hope you thanked him!"

"No, I told him to get lost. Of course I thanked him, you idiot! Anyhow, after the guy leaves, I'm about to wet my pants, being so nervous because of his gun."

"Let me guess, you had a shot of bourbon."

"No. I went and took a leak!"

"Will wonders never cease?"

"When I came back up front, I discovered that Mr. Chicago had left his black satchel. He'd set it on the floor next to the table where my cash register is, and apparently forgot about it. I was so rattled by his visit, I didn't remember it being there, either."

"Did he come back for it?"

"No! I've still got the thing!"

"Well, maybe he got lucky at Bertha's, due to his haircut."

"Corky, do you think I should hang on to it, or should I give it to the sheriff?"

"Now, why would you want to give anything to Sheriff Drew? He doesn't know what day it is most of the time. Anyhow, he'd probably accuse you of stealing it, and lock you up just so he could say he apprehended a dangerous criminal."

"I never thought of that, but you're right. Old numb-nuts would jump at the chance to be one-up on me."

"You best hang on to it, Travis. My money is

on the guy coming back for it."

"I'm thinking about heading over to Bertha's, to see if he might be hanging around there."

"Travis, don't lose any sleep over it. He'll show up."

"You're probably right. I'm just not used to somebody like him being in my shop, let alone here in Palmer Lake, where nothing ever happens."

"Listen, I've got to head home and get to bed early. I've got a job first thing in the morning. I'll talk at you later, Travis."

"Okay, Corky, have a good one."

Travis told me later that after I left, and he shut off all the lights, standing there in the dark made him feel uncomfortable.

He decided to head over to Bertha's, anyway. He was kind of afraid that the guy would think he hid his satchel on purpose. Being from a big city like Chicago, Travis figured he probably didn't understand how a small town ticks.

Palmer Lake is not what you would call self-sustaining. We feed off of Keselburg, a much larger city to the west of us about twenty miles. Several of our town folk drive there for work. Travis is always saying that the urban cave dwellers from Keselburg head our direction on the weekends to party at the lake, because slumming with the locals is their favorite past time.

When he got to Bertha's, the first place he went looking for Mr. Chicago was at the tables in

TROUBLE COMES TO PALMER LAKE

the back corner. That area is dimly lit by a faint glow of green light from the restroom sign. But he didn't find him at those tables, or in the men's room, either. So, he decided to camp out on his favorite barstool, where he could keep watch.

Chapter Three

Spending the evening at Travis's get-together was just what I needed. After a day of repairing toilets, there's nothing better than an evening of beer and checkers with the guys to help erase the memories. The story telling session was a new twist, and Travis's tale about the stranger from Chicago was pretty weird, too.

I got to know Travis when I first arrived in Palmer Lake. I stopped in for a haircut, and he filled me in on what went on around town, making it sound like a radio commercial. He even invited me to come to Pop's Saloon to listen to him play music.

Being a musician myself, I sat there listening till I couldn't take it anymore. I ran outside to my truck and grabbed my harmonicas, then joined him on stage. We both knew a lot of the same songs and we spent the rest of the night playing for the crowd.

Tonight when I got home from the get-together,

TROUBLE COMES TO PALMER LAKE

I was greeted by the blinking red light on my answering machine. It was a bit late to be returning calls, but a message from one of my customers sounded urgent, so I dialed her number.

"Is this my friend Corky the handyman, who knows better than to keep me up late waiting for the phone to ring?"

"Sorry, Colleen. I just got home. What can I do for you?"

"I've got a customer referral for you, and I expect you to treat these people like royalty."

"I'm not sure I'd know how to spread myself that thin. You're the only royalty on my list."

"Sweetheart, flattery will get you everywhere with me, but don't abuse the privilege."

"You've always encouraged me to abuse you, Colleen."

"Get your mind out of the gutter, Corky. We need to get serious for once."

"That's no fun!"

"These people want to fix up their horse barn. I mentioned you in conversation, telling them about the work you've done for us, and how you always get it right the first time."

"So, in other words, I've got to live up to some shiny reputation kind of thing, so it doesn't put a stain on yours, right?"

"It might cost you if you don't, darling. How would you like to walk with a limp the rest of your life?"

"I love it when you threaten me! Now, who the heck is so important? This is Palmer Lake, after all."

"You hit the nail right on the head, Corky. This job is for none other than Aaron Palmer, himself."

"The guy who owns Palmer Industries?"

"One and the same, sweetie."

"Since when do you and Ron hang out with a guy like that?"

"We did a Santa and Mrs. Claus dinner party appearance at his house last Christmas. After everybody there had a little too much to drink, they actually became almost normal. Ron, or I mean Santa, even had Mrs. Palmer sitting on his lap, telling him what she wanted for Christmas. She kept asking for a Nicky doll, whatever the hell that is."

"And you told all these drunks about me? That must have been the highlight of the party!"

"I admit, I puffed you up a bit. But, we got a call today from Mary Ellen Smythe, Mayor Bartholomew's secretary. The mayor wanted to know how to contact the handyman we mentioned at the Christmas party. Seems he offered to track you down, as a favor to Aaron Palmer."

"Doesn't Aaron Palmer live in Keselburg?"

"Not anymore. After he got married, he had a big place built south of town in the county. His wife wanted horses, and Keselburg wasn't the place for that."

"No kidding. Whores, maybe, but not horses."

"Would you please not talk like that, Corky, when it's me on the phone!"

"Well, maybe you better put Ron on. I'm sure it won't bother him!"

"Nothing would bother Ron right now. He's asleep in his chair with both TV sets on. One for his left brain, the other for his right."

"I won't even ask."

"So, sweetie, can you come by tomorrow? I'll give you directions to the Palmers' house. It's out there a-ways, and I wouldn't want you to get lost, anymore than you already are."

"I wouldn't miss out on a chance to see you, Colleen. I'll even put on clean underwear!"

"That's more like the Corky I know. Always showing me respect by dressing up for special events."

"You taught me well."

"If only that were true. Then we wouldn't have to wait till after dark to talk."

"Still got neighbors watching your every move?"

"This is Palmer Lake, Corky."

"Ten-four, good buddy."

"So, I'll see your smiling face tomorrow, then?"

"I'll be there in the morning around eight."

"Good night, Corky."

Colleen is a very special friend. She has kept

me busy on several home repair projects of her own, and has referred me to everyone she knows in town, as well. She is one grand lady.

I was glad there were no other messages on my answering machine tonight. I was tired, and I really didn't want to have to return any more calls.

I spent a few minutes petting my cat, then undressed and fell into bed. I was thinking about Travis's tale of Mr. Chicago, while trying to recall if I'd ever heard of anyone named Sherry Winter. Apparently, all that thinking put me to sleep.

Chapter Four

When I woke up the next morning, I had to hurry to get ready. I grabbed my clothes off the floor, laced up my boots, and had to forget about the clean undies. I told Colleen that I would stop by her place around eight and it was already quarter till!

I made it to her house in five minutes flat, only to find out that she wasn't home! There was an envelope taped to the door with my name on it, and inside were the directions to the Palmers' house, along with an apology. Seems her and Ron had a date with another couple to play pinochle that morning, and she had forgotten all about it. At least I was off the hook on the clean underwear thing!

The drive out to the Palmers' place was a long, peaceful journey. I passed acres of open land, lots of trees, and even some wildlife. Here and there I would see an occasional house, all of which were old. Most had small barns or detached garages, and no shortage of rusty old cars and trucks scattered about.

My favorite house was the one with the Porch Piglet. That's a gal who sits out front on an old sofa, wearing a tee shirt and cut-offs, smoking a cigarette and brushing her butt-length, bleached-blonde hair. Seeing her reminded me of a joke about keeping flies off the watermelon. Too bad Travis wasn't with me. This gal would have taken his mind off Mr. Chicago, for sure!

As I continued on towards the Palmers', I couldn't help but think that their barn should probably just be torn down, based on the condition of all the barns I was seeing on my drive.

I finally came to Thomas Road, where I turned and started watching mailboxes for the Palmers' address. I only had to go about a quarter-mile before I came to 24633, the address shown on Colleen's directions. I immediately realized that something was very out of place for this part of the county.

Their mailbox was stainless steel, bulletproof, and oversized, and the post was decorated with little figures of horses. Their white-painted rail fence went for as far as my eyes could see. The circular drive in front of their house was paved, not dirt, and it even had a pond in the middle of it, with a fountain!

The house was a brick two-story with a front

porch big enough to park a moving van on. There was a huge green lawn, recently mown, with underground sprinklers watering everything in sight, including a putting green. The landscaping had all kinds of trees and plants, and lots of little statues of fairies.

Just when I thought I'd seen it all, I got out of my truck and heard it all, too. There was classical music coming from speakers made to look like big rocks, and when I rang their doorbell, it played a tune that reminded me of the seventh inning stretch at a baseball stadium.

I'm used to working for people in the Palmer Lake area who have small houses, cabins, and mobile homes. Most of my customers don't even have doorbells. Usually the family dog announces my arrival. Now I understood what Colleen was referring to when she said to treat these folks like royalty!

A minute or so went by before the hand-carved wood door opened. I was greeted by a gal who looked to be in her mid-thirties, and so clean and polished, I wondered if she spent all her time in the tub. Not a hair was out of place, and she had a figure that wasn't bloated by booze and a diet of deep-fried. And it was plain to see she didn't shop at the thrift store for her clothing, like the women of Palmer Lake.

"Oh, hi there! You must be the handyman!"

"Corky Perkins, at your service."

"I'm Anita! Won't you come in? We can talk here in the entry."

And what an entry it was! There were two couches, three easy chairs, several small tables with lamps, and to top it off, a grand piano! Other than the piano, it kind of reminded me of the waiting room at the VD clinic in Keselburg. I replaced a urinal in the men's room there a few months ago, after some married guy went into a tirade and broke the thing to pieces.

"Thank you for being on time, Corky. I have a riding lesson in a half-hour, and my instructor is never late. If you will drive your truck down to the barn, I can show you what I want done. Just follow the gravel lane that runs along the fence, and I'll meet you down there in a couple minutes, after I change into my riding outfit."

The gravel lane was easily a quarter-mile long, and it ended at a great-looking barn! I was wrong, thinking it needed to be torn down. In fact, I couldn't imagine the place needing any kind of an overhaul!

After the long drive out to their place, I was about to burst. I decided to relieve myself behind the barn, and was almost done when I heard Anita's voice in the distance.

"Corky, are you here? Corky, it's me, Anita! Where are you, Corky? I see your truck, but I don't see you! Corky the handyman, where are you?"

"I'm over here."

"Oh, there you are! What are you doing back there?"

"Just looking around."

"Corky, we'll have to make this quick. I've got my list right here. The first thing I want, are hooks all along that wall. I never have enough hooks!

"Then, down here on this wall, I want one of those little cat doors. My barn cat needs her own entrance. Make sure it's not mounted up too high, or she'll have trouble getting in and out!

"Over here, I want you to put a switch that will turn on an overhead light up there. I need it to be a red floodlight that shines down on these shelves. I reached up there to get the cat food and a mouse jumped out from behind the cans! It scared me so bad, I screamed!"

"A red floodlight?"

"Yes! Mice don't like red light!"

"I didn't know that. Okay, one mouse light, a cat door, and some wall hooks. Anything else?"

"Corky, honestly! I brought a long list!"

"What else is on it?"

"Do you see that water pipe? It goes through the wall to a faucet on the outside. It freezes up in the winter, and I want that fixed!

"Over on this wall, I want a window put in, so I can watch the boy that shovels our horse manure. He always makes such a mess! If I can see him doing it when I'm in here, then I can go speak to him!"

"You really do have quite a list."

"Yes, I do. But I need to get ready for my riding lesson, so we'll have to continue later. You can start with the little things right now. The hooks and the cat door are in a bag over there by that big box.

"Oh, here comes my instructor! I have to go! Watch out for my barn kitty, so she doesn't get hurt!"

I could say that Anita was fascinating, but I'm not sure that would be accurate. She has this organizational quality about her, yet she seems sort of distant from reality somehow. Maybe I'm just not used to being around a horsewoman.

I began unloading my tools from the truck, as I watched Anita and her trainer lead one of the horses past the barn to the arena. As they went by, it sounded like she was telling the trainer how it would be. I was starting to get the impression that she ran the show.

Going about my business, I installed the hooks on the wall first. Next came the cat door. That's the one I had to laugh about. The cat obviously had no problem coming and going from the barn, so what was the big deal about having to have a special door? I just did as I was told and cut the hole in the wall.

As I was finishing up installing the kitty door, I spotted Anita walking her horse past the barn again. This time she was heading back toward the pasture, and she was scolding the horse for misbehaving. Her instructor was already back at his truck, so the riding lesson must be over for the day.

A couple minutes later, I heard her voice again.

"Corky, did you find the toilet?"

"I haven't felt the need yet, but thanks for asking."

"No, stupid! The toilet! Over there, in the big box, by where you got the hooks and the cat door from!"

"What are you talking about?"

"Look, right here! This is an electric toilet for the barn!"

"Anita, toilets don't plug in like a lamp. They get plumbed in."

"You men are all alike! Read the label! Stainless steel, electric toilet, no plumbing required!"

"No shit?"

"Very funny, Corky. Ha-ha, I'm laughing."

"Where did you get this thing?"

"I ordered it from a catalog that my friend Alayne gave me. Her husband put one in their barn."

"How the heck does this thing work?"

"It burns everything up and turns it to ash. It's really good to mix the ash in with your garden soil!"

"That sure makes me hungry for a tomato."

"I want it to go in the tack room, and I also

want this new door put in for privacy. There's supposed to be a toilet paper holder with it that can store six rolls. Just hang that on the wall next to the toilet. If you can't do it, Corky, I'm going to have to find someone else."

"Well, it sounds easier than a regular toilet, if all you really have to do is plug it in. Let me read the instructions and see what it requires."

"I'm counting on you, Corky. I don't know another handyman. And I can't ask Alayne's husband to do it, not since his accident."

"What happened?"

"Their mule kicked him and broke four of his ribs!"

"What did he do to make the mule mad?"

"Nothing! The mule has been with them for several years and it just went crazy!"

"If it were me, there would have been mule stew on the table for dinner."

"Have you ever tried mule stew, Corky?"

"I think my Aunt Billie used to fix it for us, when she came to visit."

"Oh, brother! I'm going back up to the house now."

Anita stomped off like a little kid and began arguing with the invisible man. I watched as her arms started waving, and she began kicking at the gravel. I couldn't make out what she was saying, but she sure seemed ticked off!

I unpacked the toilet and began reading the

instructions. To my surprise, it really was quite a simple install process. The toilet needed to be vented to the outside, but other than that, you just bolted it down and wired it. Travis could save on his water bill if he put one of these in his barbershop, what with Toot being there every day.

I got the toilet mounted to the floor and then cut the hole in the wall for the vent pipe. I had to go outside to finish up that part of the project.

The temperature was in the mid-eighties, and I was in need of some relief from the aroma of horse manure. Before continuing with the installation, I decided to take a break. I looked around for any sign of Anita before lighting up a smoke. I didn't want to get caught and sent to the principal's office.

While enjoying my cigarette, I noticed a number of orange flags on poles in the pasture area. They were spaced about every hundred feet, and they went all the way up to the backyard of the house. I figured it must be some kind of a riding obstacle course.

As I was looking at those flags, I happened to spot Anita on her deck, talking with some guy dressed in a suit and tie. Their deck was at ground level and went all the way across the back of the house. From my vantage point, I couldn't really see everything that was on it, but I'm sure it included all the best, like a hot tub and a barbecue.

All of a sudden, Anita started shouting! The

horses in the pasture stopped eating and raised their heads to see what the noise was. The guy turned and started walking away from her, but she followed, with arms waving frantically. They headed around the side of the house and out of sight.

I lit up another smoke and continued watching to see what might happen next. A few seconds later, I heard tires squealing and could just see the tail end of a black car heading out of the circular driveway.

I watched for another five minutes, but nothing more happened, so I decided to get back to work.

The toilet was almost ready to go, except for finishing the electrical hook-up. It required a dedicated twenty-amp circuit, which meant I would have to install an additional circuit breaker. Since the toilet didn't come with one, I would have to pick that up at the hardware store, along with the red mouse light.

I got a good start on Anita's list, but really couldn't go any further without the supplies. So, I loaded my tools into the truck, and headed up the gravel lane towards their house.

I was going to tell Anita where things stood with the barn projects, but at the last moment, I chose not to. I didn't want her screaming at me about the toilet not being finished, and chasing me off like the other guy.

I left the Palmers' driveway and got back on the road. It was still really hot out, and with no air conditioning in my truck, I had to keep wiping the sweat off my forehead. That got me to thinking about stopping at Bertha's for a cold beer. So, I pushed on the accelerator and passed the Porch Piglet's place doing sixty-five!

Chapter Five

When I arrived at Bertha's, there were almost no parking spots left. Normally, finding a place to park could be done blindfolded. This heat wave must have affected the whole town.

Inside, I couldn't believe how many people were there. Then it hit me - the air conditioner was on! I spotted Travis sitting on his favorite barstool, so I headed over.

"Welcome to paradise, Corky."

"Travis, what the hell brings you here this evening? Let me guess-your motorcycle!"

"You know, Corky, one thing never changes - you're always a smart-ass. But I guess someone's got to hold the job!"

"Hey, Travis, you'll never guess where my travels have led me to now."

"Let's see, if I know you as well as I think I do, you followed your nose and it led you to another plugged-up toilet."

"You're good, Travis. Now, see if you can elaborate."

"I never elaborate in public, Corky. It's against the law."

"What?"

"I saw a guy elaborate on the sidewalk once. The cops came and hauled him off."

"Travis, how many have you had?"

"I'm just pulling your chain, Corky. You take things too seriously sometimes. Why don't you just tell me where you've been working at? I'm too worn out from the heat to play games. And what about that drink you're going to buy me?"

"I didn't know I'd offered."

I signaled Bertha to bring us some liquid refreshment. Travis was having bourbon, while I ordered up an ice-cold beer. I needed something to wash down the taste of the barn.

"Travis, do you know anything about Aaron Palmer?"

"Corky, everybody in town knows who he is."

"I know that, but do you know him personally at all?"

"I've cut his hair once or twice, but I don't know anything about him other than he owns Palmer Industries."

"Do you know his wife?"

"His wife? Oh, yeah, sure. I take her for rides on my motorcycle, and we go to the motel a couple times a week."

"Travis, I'm serious, do you know his wife or not?"

"I've heard that he married some young gal who isn't from around here. But other than that, I wouldn't know her if I woke up next to her."

"Well, I started a job out at their place today. Let me tell you, this is some kind of pad they live in!"

"I thought you said you weren't going to take any more jobs in Keselburg, after the clinic job that my sister turned you on to."

"They don't live in Keselburg. He had this big place built out in the south part of the county area."

"The south county area? That's full of pig farmers and ugly women! I was out there once when I first moved to Palmer Lake. I made a left turn by mistake. Are you telling me his wife's so ugly that he has to keep her hidden there?"

"It isn't like that at all, Travis. She's a looker."

"A what?"

"A good-looking woman."

"Oh, I thought you said she was a hooker!"

"I think you've reached your limit for the evening, Travis."

"Don't start, Corky. I'm a big boy. Just ask any of the women in Palmer Lake."

"No, thanks. As was I saying before I was so rudely interrupted, Mrs. Palmer is good looking.

Her name is Anita."

"Sounds like a hooker's name to me."

"Travis, maybe you haven't had enough to drink!"

I raised my hand and signaled to Bertha again. She wasted no time bringing us another round. I think she had them ready and was just waiting for the wave. Travis has always been a little afraid of her because of things like that. He's told me more than once she has ESP.

"So, Travis, you must be here to cool off in the air conditioning. Did you close up early?"

"There wasn't anyone in the barbershop all day except Toot. I got tired of playing checkers, so I locked up at two o'clock and came here on the chance that I might find Mr. Chicago."

"Still a no show?"

"Yep. Bertha thinks I'm making this whole thing up about him and the satchel. She says there hasn't been anybody in here that fits his description. I asked the other girls waiting tables, but they haven't seen him, either."

"Have you checked anywhere besides here?"

"No. The way I figure it, a guy like him is bound to stop here. I'm betting he was either born in the ladies' room of a lounge, or conceived in the parking lot of one."

"Travis, you can't seem to let this thing go. Why is it so important that you return his satchel? I'm sure the guy will contact you sooner or later."

"Maybe you're right, but I doubt it. You've never been right before. I don't want the guy to think I swiped it."

"Hey, Travis, you'll never guess what I'm doing at the Palmer place."

"Is it for Mr. Palmer, or for his wife?"

"It's for Anita. I haven't even seen Aaron there yet."

"You fixed her toilet and now you're playing doctor with her."

"Not even. But you're getting warm on part of it. I'm actually installing an electric toilet in their horse barn."

"Now, since when does a horse need a toilet, Corky?"

"No, you idiot, it's for her!"

"Did I hear you right? An electric toilet? What, the thing wipes and powders her when she pushes a button?"

"Travis, at first I thought Anita was pulling my leg. Then she showed me the thing. It's for real!"

"Was she pulling your third leg?"

"No, she didn't pull my third leg! She showed me the electric toilet and told me to install it in the tack room."

"Corky, even I know that water and electricity don't mix."

"It doesn't use water. It burns up the pumpies and a fan blows the fumes outside."

"You think the neighbors will like that?"

"Like what?"

"Being down wind!"

"I doubt if anyone around there would even notice. They all have animals. One guy even has a mule that kicked him and broke four of his ribs!"

"An electric toilet - what will they think of next? Is it coin-operated, like the kiddy rides out front of the grocery store in Keselburg?"

"Hey, Travis, that's a good idea! Maybe you can order a coin operated model for the barbershop to help pay the rent."

"Maybe you should put a quarter in it and flush yourself up in smoke!"

"I've got to get some stuff at the hardware store tomorrow to finish up the job. Maybe they'll be able to tell me how to hook the thing up so it vibrates. That would sure surprise Anita!"

"Since she's one of those women with lots of money, it doesn't sound like her idea of fun, Corky."

"Travis, I think her idea of fun is arguing."

"That's how all women are!"

"Yeah, but this gal is really different."

"They're all different, Corky. But they're all the same, too. Trust me."

"No, Anita has a bolt loose or something. She was lippy with me, lippy with her riding instructor, and lippy with her horse. A little bit later, I saw her arguing with some guy in a suit and tie on her back deck. She wound up chasing the guy off and screaming so loud, the horses were even spooked!"

"Okay, I think I've heard enough about Mrs. Money Bags."

"You want to talk about Mr. Chicago, don't you?"

"Corky, this thing is really bugging me. I know that something must have happened to him, or he'd have picked up his satchel by now. Nobody takes me seriously when I bring it up. Even Toot said I should just play checkers and not think about it. But I'm the one who has the damn thing!"

"Maybe the guy had to leave town unexpectedly."

"When it comes to smelling trouble, Corky, I've developed quite a nose. One reason I came to Palmer Lake was to get away from trouble. It used to follow me around like a dog. I'm starting to have those old feelings again, like something's nipping at my heels."

"Travis, I've never seen you like this."

"Corky, I've got a hell of a headache. I think I'll head home and call it a day."

Travis took off and left me at Bertha's to fend for myself. I thought the electric toilet story would keep him entertained for hours, but that satchel was all he could think about. Too bad he left so soon, because the Buettemeier sisters showed up.

Pinkie and Rosie are regulars at Bertha's, and Travis always has interesting things to say about them. He told me that both of the girls had been married before, but now they prefer to share a man between them. Travis has such a hard time pronouncing their last name that he just refers to them as the Buttmores'.

One of my fantasies is to hang out with those girls and see if everything I've heard about them is really true. But, I'll have to wait for another day, because they just sat down at a booth with Billy Hamrod. Rosie started rubbing his shoulders and Pinkie was hand-feeding him chips.

I finished my beer and decided to head for home, rather than watch those three continue to play grab-ass. Anyway, I needed to get all rested up for another day of fun with Anita!

Chapter Six

When I woke up the next morning, the first thought that came to mind had to do with the smell of horse manure. Maybe I could find some high-powered air freshener at the hardware store.

My goals for the day were to finish the electric toilet wiring and install the red mouse light. Time permitting, I might get the privacy door installed, as well. Anita probably needed that more than anything, so she didn't spook the horses!

Once I finally got on the road, my first stop was our local hardware store, where I used to work. They had every fragrance of air freshener known to man, but not the brand of circuit breaker I needed. Their choice of light fixtures was fairly decent, but wouldn't you know, they were out of red floodlights!

That meant I was going to have to make a trip

to Jumbo's Hardware in Keselburg, which would eat up most of my day. As much as I liked Jumbo's, there wouldn't be any point trying to get anything done at the Palmers', because it would be too late.

I went back home to call Anita and give her the bad news. I dialed her number, let it ring ten times, and got no answer. I waited five minutes and tried again, and still no answer. How come they didn't have an answering machine? If I could afford one, they certainly could!

I got back in my truck and decided to head to Keselburg. I figured I'd take my chances with Anita. It wouldn't surprise me if she fired me and refused to pay for what I'd done so far!

Jumbo's had everything I needed, plus I found something to add to my collection. It was called a pick-up tool, and according to the label, it's made for grabbing things that are a little out of reach. I planned to try it out at Bertha's when the Buettemeier sisters came in. That should make Travis sit up and take notice!

While I spent my day shopping at Jumbo's, Travis was hosting another Senior Citizen's Day at the barbershop. He did this once a month as his way of appearing to be a great guy. It didn't amount to a lot of money, but he did see a few more customers on this special day. One thing he's learned about seniors in Palmer Lake is a few of them are a real pain in the ass. You would think at their age they would have mellowed out, but he still sees the two or three who think their seat reverberations don't stink.

Travis still had Mr. Chicago on the brain when his first customer of the day, the distinguished attorney himself, Morgan B. Claymore, arrived. Claymore began his legal studies when he was in the military and went into private practice after he retired as a colonel. Town folk say that old Morgan could have taken Clarence Darrow through a refresher course in any courtroom in the land.

To a certain degree, Travis enjoyed chatting with Claymore when he cut his hair. Claymore could talk up a storm on most any subject, law or otherwise. It seemed to irritate him, though, when Travis addressed him by his initials, M.B. He did that when Claymore got too high and mighty. Travis's favorite line when talking about Claymore's visit is always, "This is my barbershop, and he needs to remember who's holding the razor!"

"Morning, your honor. I see you are first in line again on Senior's Day."

"Travis O'Riley, I've come to swear you in as the official barber of Palmer Lake."

This was the same old line that Claymore always greeted Travis with. Just once, he would have liked to hear him say something different. But, that's what seniors mean by being regular.

"I accept the nomination, your honor. Now, what do I win?"

"Travis O'Riley, you win the right to practice

an honest day's work in Palmer Lake, serving your fellow citizens."

As many times as Travis participated in this routine, he should have had a shelf full of awards. However, his only shelf was in the bathroom, full of rolls of toilet paper for the seniors.

"M.B., I was wondering if you'd crossed paths with any strangers in town?"

"You mean, stranger than you and I?"

"You've got me there! But seriously, have you run into a guy from Chicago?"

"No, can't say as I've met up with any strangers lately. Why do you ask?"

"Well, this guy stopped in for a haircut a few days ago. He didn't talk much, and kind of gave me the cold shoulder. But, he left his satchel here and he still hasn't picked the thing up."

"Well, just hang on to it, he'll be back."

"That's what everyone tells me."

"Say, did I mention that the mayor has been catching his limit every trip out? I'm heading down to his boat this morning to see if I can be so lucky. Thanks for the trim, Travis. See you in a month."

Nobody seemed to care much about the predicament Travis had been put in with that satchel. We all just thought it was no big deal.

Travis had three more old timers stop in before lunchtime. He was having a hard time concentrating on cutting hair, because he couldn't quit thinking about Mr. Chicago. And being forced to listen to conversations about laxatives didn't help, either.

In less than two shakes of a dead cat's tail, he headed across the street to the Bite Time Café, where he always eats lunch. The Bite Time is the official gossip place of the local residents, and Travis was figuring on asking some the locals if they had seen Mr. Chicago. The owner, Sally Henderson, is the queen of gossip. She started as a waitress there, but wound up buying the place after she received insurance money from her husband's death.

Travis sat down on his favorite stool at the far end of the counter and spotted several familiar faces. At a table in back was Mary Ellen Smythe, eating her usual tuna salad with a side order of romance novel. Up in front by the windows was Toot, sitting at the same table as Birdman, who had one of his parrots on his shoulder.

Travis had only been seated for a minute when Sally poured him a cup of coffee.

"How are you, Travis?"

"Confused as always, Sally. How's biz?"

"You know what they say, chicken one day and feathers the next."

"So, what is it today?"

"More feathers than chicken today. What can I get for you?"

"What's the special?"

"Travis, today we're proud to be serving meatloaf surprise."

"Really? What's the surprise?"

TROUBLE COMES TO PALMER LAKE

"It comes with a side order of stomach trouble."

"I'll give it a try. Nothing from your kitchen has killed me so far!"

"Well, Travis, that might be part of the surprise, too!"

Travis grabbed his coffee and headed over to Toot and Birdman's table. He hadn't seen Birdman since the barbershop get-together.

"Birdie, did you bring your parrot to have lunch, or to have for lunch?"

"Very funny, Travis. You ever consider a career in comedy?"

"Yeah, once upon a time I did. But, as it turned out, I was more of a joke than a joker!"

"How they hanging, Travis?"

"Lefty and Righty are just fine, Toot."

"Travis, pull up a chair and sit a spell. My bird could use a clean shoulder."

At that point, Travis had to restrain himself from telling Birdman the one about the roasted parrot on a Kaiser roll. Birdie didn't find humor in those kinds of jokes.

"Travis O'Riley, your meatloaf surprise awaits! Are you going to sit over there with your feathered friends, or do you want me to put it at the counter?"

"You're welcome to eat here with me and Toot, Travis. You don't have to sit up there all alone, feeling sorry for yourself."

"Sally, I'll be dining with these two gents."

"That's going to cost extra for the delivery service!"

"Birdman said he'd leave you a tip."

"As long as it's not the bird leaving it! Here's your meatloaf surprise, Travis, complete with a bottle of tummy syrup."

"That's pretty funny, Sally."

"Who's being funny?"

"Hey, Sally, have you noticed any strangers around the old choke-and-puke lately?"

"I see an occasional stranger in here now and then. Why do you ask?"

"Well, I'm curious as to whether anyone in town has seen a guy from Chicago."

"What did he do, refuse to pay for his haircut?"

"No, quite the opposite. He tipped me ten bucks!"

"Ten dollars? You must be feeling guilty! Are you going to give him a refund?"

"Listen, Sally, could you be serious for a minute? This guy came in for a haircut, but he forgot his satchel and he still hasn't come back for it."

"What's in the satchel, more ten dollar bills?"

"I have no idea, and I'm not about to go snooping."

"You know, now that you mention it, I did see a stranger in here early one morning this week. What did the guy look like?"

"He was over six feet tall, slender, and dressed very well."

"That sounds a lot like the guy. He was tall and handsome, and looked like he had money. I was hoping he wanted me to run away with him!"

"Did you talk to him?"

"That's the funny part. I tried to start up a conversation, but he didn't want to chat. He just sat there quietly and ate his breakfast."

"That sounds like the guy, alright. Has he been back in?"

"Unfortunately not. I like the tall ones."

"Tall ones, short ones, it doesn't matter to you, Sally, as long as they have money! If you happen to see him again, would you send him my direction?"

"I will, if you will."

"If I will, what?"

"Send him my direction, silly!"

Travis finished his meatloaf surprise and was ready to get back to work cutting more seniors. As he was about to leave, Birdman kicked the leg of his chair.

"Travis, I couldn't help overhearing you and Sally talk about the stranger. You said he's from Chicago?"

"That's what he told me. Why?"

"At work, one of the guards told me about a guy who's been trying to get in to see Mr. Palmer without an appointment. The guy gets pissed off cause we won't let him in and he keeps threatening my guard."

"What did your guard do?"

"He radioed for help, and when the other guards arrived, the guy took off."

"Really? When's the last time he was there?"

"Not for a couple of days, now. But, Travis, I'm wondering if he might be the guy from Chicago that you were talking about? The guard described him as tall, and dressed in a suit and tie."

"Well, if he shows up again, send him over to my barbershop. I'm getting tired of babysitting his damn satchel!"

Travis grabbed the tummy syrup and waved good-bye to Sally, then headed back to his shop.

Chapter Seven

Yesterday, I spent most of my day driving to Keselburg and back, instead of getting more work done at the barn. I had planned on doing several of the jobs, so Anita would smile for once, but I must have been dreaming.

In the evening, Travis and I got together at Bertha's, where he filled me in about Senior's Day, complete with a detailed description of popular laxatives. He seems to think I need to know about them because I repair toilets.

Today, I was back on the road again, heading to the Palmers'. During my drive, I got to see a mother duck and her six little ones waddle across the road to a pond. I was happy to wait and watch, since the only waddling I ever see in Palmer Lake is in a pair of stretch pants, two sizes too small!

Before long, I was at Anita's driveway, and I drove straight down the gravel lane to the barn without stopping at the house. I assumed I'd be in trouble for not showing up yesterday, so why waste time being punished? I could be making progress.

On my last visit, I had gotten the toilet mounted and vented, and I had run the wiring over to the breaker box. Now, I just needed to install the new circuit breaker and connect the wires to it. Since the cover was still off the box, it would only take a few minutes to complete. Then I could proceed with the burn tests to see if Anita's high-tech shitter was a go.

When I got to the breaker panel, I damn near dropped my toolbox! Someone had fooled around with the toilet wires, and had connected them directly to the main power lugs in the breaker box! Not only that, the wires were hooked up in reverse! What idiot would do such a thing?

I unhooked the faulty wiring connections, installed the new circuit breaker, and reattached the wires correctly. Thanks to some jerk, it wound up taking me three times as long as it should have!

The instructions that came with the electric toilet said to perform a burn test using toilet paper first to make sure the heating element and the vent fan worked properly. I opened the package of TP that Anita had left with all of the other goodies, unrolled a few feet, and lifted the lid. That's when I found surprise number two!

I'd been concerned that horse manure would fog my brain again today, but I would have settled for horse in a heartbeat!

I didn't stop at the house the other day to let Anita know I wasn't able to finish wiring the toilet. She was so anxious to get the thing installed, she must have come back after I was gone and gave it a try. No wonder I hadn't seen Mrs. Lincoln Log at the barn this morning! She must have had her riding instructor or one of the lawn guys try hooking up the wires so she could incinerate her embarrassingly oversized load!

I started looking around for something to remove the pile with, and a container of some kind to put it in. I had to get that stuff out of the toilet so I could perform the burn test with the TP. I grabbed a pair of hay tongs that were hanging on the wall, and some pink rubber boots off the shelf.

I held my breath and lifted the lid again, and used the tongs to carefully transfer the hidden treasure into the boots. Had the boots been a size smaller, they wouldn't have held it all. Now, if the electric toilet passed its first burn test using the paper, at least I'd have the more substantial fuel I needed for the second test.

I was very impressed with how the toilet heated up. It incinerated the paper, while the fan blew the smoke and fumes outside.

Now it was time for the number-two test. I emptied the contents of the boots back into the toilet and hit the switch. Unfortunately, it took a lot longer for that stuff to burn up. I had to check the vent system during each test, and the first time, with the toilet paper, it was no big deal. The second test changed my haircut from a comb-over to a flattop.

As soon as I was done, I hung up the tongs and put the rubber boots back on the shelf. After finding the faulty wiring, and the surprise under the lid, I felt like I got screwed over on this toilet deal. Using Anita's pink boots was my way of trying to even the score.

After all of that, I went outside and lit up a smoke. While I was standing there, I heard a voice. It wasn't Anita - she could be heard loud and clear from a quarter-mile off. It sounded more like a man's voice, but it was so distant, I couldn't make out what he was saying. There was a wooded area behind the barn a few hundred feet, and I figured that maybe he was walking his dog in there. I kept listening, but I didn't hear anything more.

I finished my cigarette and went back to work. Anita had left me her list, and there seemed to be more on it than I remembered. She made a big deal out of some of the items, like the toilet and the mouse light, but there were plenty more she hadn't brought up. It looked like I was going to be hanging around for longer than I figured.

It had gotten pretty hot again, and that kind of zapped my energy. In between some of the jobs, I would take a break and go talk to the horses. The strangest thing kept happening, though. Every time I'd mention Anita's name, the one male horse would lift his leg!

It was getting to be late in the afternoon, and I still hadn't seen Anita. That was really strange, given her need to control every detail of the barn renovation.

For my last job of the day, I hung up the giant toilet paper holder. Anita was right - the thing really did hold six rolls. Judging from the size of her contribution, she was going to need all six!

Chapter Eight

I had no plans of stopping at Bertha's on the way home from the Palmers', but the heat got to me again, and I made the decision to go have a cold beer.

The parking lot was packed. Out front on the sidewalk I spotted Pinkie and Rosie, playing kissing games with Billy Hamrod. Inside, about half of the town's population had arrived. There were even some of the older folks there. The air conditioning must make Bertha a ton of money!

I was hoping I would run into Travis, so I could tell him about the surprise that Anita had left me. And there he was, on his favorite barstool, engaged in conversation with Lindsey the waitress.

Lindsey and Travis shared a special moment at Bertha's early one afternoon last week. He had stopped in when there weren't any other customers, and spotted Lindsey setting tables. He quietly snuck up on her and said, "Boo!" She let out a scream, which he expected. But she also let out a two-cheek-sneak that even a long-haul trucker would have been proud of! Ever since, she has been begging Travis not to tell anyone about her trumpeting.

As I approached the two of them from behind, I couldn't resist announcing myself.

"Boo!"

"What the hell? Corky!"

"Sorry to butt in on your fun, you two."

"Hey, Lindsey, don't run away! Corky, she's going to kick my ass for that!"

"Travis, when are you going to understand that she doesn't want anything to do with your ass?"

"Well, you sure took care of any chance I had!"

"I think her daddy would see to that, when he finds out you've been sniffing."

"What do you know about her daddy, smart boy?"

"I know that Lindsey still lives at home."

"Corky, you're just saying that because I saw her first."

"Travis, I worked at their house last winter replacing their basement stairs. I'm sure you've driven past it. It's the one that has the Risvold's Septic Pumping truck parked out front."

"Denny Risvold?"

"One and the same."

"You're telling me that Lindsey is his daughter?"

"If you don't believe me, ask Bertha."

"I think I will. Bertha! Hey, Bertha!"

"What is it, Travis? Is your glass empty?"

"Bertha, what's Lindsey's last name?"

"You mean my waitress, Lindsey? It's Risvold."

"No fooling?"

"Is that all you need, Travis? I'm kind of busy at the moment."

"That's all. Thanks, Bertha."

"Now do you believe me?"

"I had no idea she was his kid!"

"Relax, Travis. A waitress in a bar might as well be wearing a For Rent sign on her back."

"I never thought of it like that."

"Hey, you'll never guess what kind of a surprise Anita left me today."

"A pair of her panties in your tool box?"

"I hope not. Those damp things would rust my pliers! Anyhow, I don't think she wears any. The surprise was under the lid of the electric toilet."

"You're not saying what I think you're saying, are you?"

"Just picture Toot's dam busting after he held it for a week."

"You told me that toilet burns everything up!"

"It does. But Anita used it before I had the electricity connected."

TROUBLE COMES TO PALMER LAKE

"Did she fess up?"

"Nope. I think she's too embarrassed. In fact, I didn't see her at all today."

"Corky, I was telling Old Man Stranoder that you're working out at the Palmer place, and he said that Leroy and Mama Lacome live right next door to them."

"Who's Old Man Stranoder?"

"I've told you about him before. He's the only guy in Palmer Lake with a swimming pool."

"Oh, him. Well, I've never paid any attention to who lives next door. The Palmer place is so big, compared to all the others around there, it's kind of its own world."

"He said they live on the other side of the fence that runs along the gravel road to the barn. I guess he goes out there every so often to visit Leroy."

"I'll have to take a look."

"I guess the place is a real eyesore."

"Travis, that's fashionable out in the south county area."

"Stranoder calls it Corn-Hole County."

"And he's a senior citizen?"

"Corky, some stuff has been going on for a lot longer than you or I have been alive!"

"Travis, I need to get home and wash some clothes tonight, so I'm only going to have one beer."

"That's okay by me. I don't think I'm going to hang around here either, after learning about Lindsey Risvold."

"Given the Lindsey disappointment, do I dare ask about Mr. Chicago?"

"Still a no show. But I did hear from the Birdman that a guy matching his description was out at Palmer Industries causing trouble. At least that's something."

"Well, something's better than nothing!"

"Corky, I'm trying to remember if one of my van girls was named Sherry Winter?"

"Don't you have them sign your guest book?"

"Now, there's an idea."

"That's what I'd do if I had a van!"

"So, Corky, how do you know Anita doesn't wear panties?"

Travis and I finished our drinks and then made our way out to the parking lot. He climbed on his motorcycle, I climbed in my truck, and the Buettemeier girls climbed on Billy Hamrod in the back seat of his car.

Chapter Nine

After leaving Bertha's, I stayed up late doing my laundry. My work clothes always come out of the washer looking about the same as they do going in. But, I have to wash my shorts a couple of times with bleach, to knock out the rainbow effect.

When one of my jobs takes longer than a day or two, I start feeling like an employee again. That's why remodels are my least favorite. The Palmer barn job was a far cry from a remodel, but I was starting to feel that anxious little tick the next morning. Maybe it was just the thought of running into Anita, and having to discuss turds in a business-like manner.

I really enjoy the drive out to their place. It's long enough to be able to listen to most any tape in my collection. This morning's selection was the Mystic album, by the Troublemakers. I like to play their music real loud!

I finally made the turn onto Thomas Road, and then got to the Palmers' driveway. I wanted to drive real slow on my way to the barn so I could check out the place next door where Leroy and Mama Lacome live.

Sure enough, there was a dumpy little house on the other side of the fence. There was even a garage out back with a bunch of old faded gas station signs hanging on it. The garage was leaning quite a bit and there was mold growing up one side. And, like all the other places out that way, there was a collection of broken-down, rusty vehicles scattered about.

Leroy and Mama own and operate the one and only service station in Palmer Lake. Leroy fills your tank and washes your windshield, and Mama runs the cash register while watching her little black-and-white TV. If people want a modern, shiny place to fill up, they have to go all the way to Keselburg. The Lacomes' station is pretty filthy, so it's best not to use the restroom!

Anita's barn upgrades included a number of fluorescent lights she bought to replace the regular bulb-type fixtures. She had written a note to me that said the new lights would help cut down on the flies. I think her leftovers were more to blame for the fly problem!

I strapped on my tool belt, climbed up the ladder, and started installing the new lights. After about an hour, I started smelling something. One never knows what might cause a bad odor in a horse barn. But, as time passed, and the temperature got warmer, the unfamiliar smell continued to get stronger. So, I climbed down the ladder to see if I could locate the source.

My first thought was to check the electric toilet. I could only imagine what I might find in there this time! I gloved up and put on my dust mask, prepared for the worst. I slowly lifted the lid, but found myself staring at an empty bowl. Then I went around back to where the vent pipe came through the wall. Being the brave handyman that I am, I bent down and took a sniff. Nothing.

Next, I made two complete trips around the outside of the barn. I did notice on the south side, where the toilet vent was, the smell seemed to be a bit stronger, but it was probably just mind over matter. I finally gave up and decided that the odor must be coming from one of the neighbor's outhouses. There certainly is no shortage of those around this part of the world!

It was getting to be lunchtime according to my stomach, so I took off my tool belt, climbed in my truck, and opened up my lunchbox. Today's meal was leftover Chinese from my trip to Keselburg yesterday. I figured I best get it eaten up before I found bugs in it like the last time. Leaving the open container on my kitchen counter overnight wasn't such a good idea!

After I finished my lunch, the day was half over. But, I had a full stomach, and getting to listen to some tunes was just what I needed to refresh myself. As I prepared to get back to work on the barn, I realized that I'd forgotten all about the mystery smell during my lunch break. Maybe the Chinese food overpowered it. Whatever had done it unfortunately wasn't doing it when I got back on the ladder!

The temperature had continued to rise, pushing the barn thermometer to ninety-three, and giving a whole new meaning to the word ripe! I figured that Anita would know where that foul smell was coming from. She's certainly a know-it-all about everything else around here. So, before I continued with anymore work, I decided to go up to the house and find out what stunk. Her poop embarrassment thing had gone on long enough!

I took the long walk up the gravel lane and noticed that the air smelled better the further I got from the barn. By the time I arrived at her driveway, I couldn't smell a thing. Maybe their septic tank was located down there somewhere, and it was leaking. Whatever it was, kind of reminded me of Bertha's bean dip birthday party last winter.

As I walked around the circular drive, I didn't hear the classical music coming from the big rock speakers. I pushed the doorbell button and listened for the baseball music. Sure enough, that was working. I stood there waiting for a couple of minutes, but no one answered. I figured Anita might have been on the phone and didn't hear me.

I pushed the button again, but still no answer. I got to thinking that she might just be in the bathroom. Judging from the size of the contribution I discovered in the electric toilet, this girl not only rides a horse, she eats like one, too!

I tried the doorbell one last time, but nobody came to greet me. So, I gave up and headed back towards the gravel lane, wondering if Anita was still too embarrassed to face me. Then, I heard a voice from across the fence.

"Hey, fella, what do you think you're doing over there?"

"Who said that?"

"I've been watching you."

"Leroy, is that you?"

"How do you know my name?"

"Leroy, it's Corky Perkins. Don't you recognize me?"

"Corky? Let me put on my glasses. By golly, it is you. What are you doing way out here?"

"I've been working on the Palmers' barn."

"You're the guy doing that?"

"I'm the lucky one."

"Corky, since when do you work on barns?"

"Since now, Leroy. This is my first one."

"I thought you worked at the hardware store."

"Leroy, those gasoline fumes must be getting to you. I only worked there for a few days, and that was a couple of years ago."

"So why are you up here snooping around the Palmers' house? The barn is down in back."

"I needed to talk to Mrs. Palmer about a problem."

"Well, you ain't going to find her at home."

"You're right. I rang the doorbell several times, but no one answered."

"You can ring that thing all you want, Corky, but the Palmers' took off on some sort of a vacation-shopping trip."

"Anita didn't tell me they were going away."

"Mr. Palmer decided to surprise her with a little out-of-town getaway. He asked me if I'd look after things and feed the animals while they're gone."

"Well, that's just great. Now I'll have to wait until they get back!"

"What kind of problem you having, Corky?"

"There's a foul smell down there, Leroy. It's been coming on strong with this heat, and it's getting pretty bad."

"I don't notice any smell around here."

"I don't notice it up here by the house, either. Down at the barn it's getting so strong, you can almost taste it."

"Must be coming from over at the Slyfield place. This time of year they butcher some of their hogs. If the weather is hot, with a little breeze, things can get to stinking."

"Where's the Slyfield place?"

"It's on the other side of those woods behind the barn."

"Maybe that's why the Palmers took off for a few days."

"I wouldn't know. Well, listen, Corky, I've got to get back to the gas station before Mama sends a posse out looking for me. If I was you, I wouldn't waste time worrying about no smell, just get the barn finished up for Miss Anita."

I started wondering why Leroy was home in the middle of the afternoon? I couldn't imagine Mama running their station by herself. She'd miss out on all of her TV shows if she did that.

I headed back to the barn, hoping the smell might have disappeared while I was away. Unfortunately, the closer I got, the more my nose started to drip. So, I decided to see if I could find the Slyfield's slaughterhouse.

I walked down to the horse arena, which was a hundred feet or so behind the barn. The smell seemed a bit stronger, so I continued on to the edge of the woods. There, I spotted the beginning of a trail that must be for riding horses, based on all the piles of manure.

I started walking the trail and had only gone in a few feet when I came to a bit of standing water. Given the heat we were having, I thought that was strange. Then, I got this crazy idea and decided to wade in it just for fun. A splash or two later, I began to wonder if the puddle was runoff from the septic tank. Now I felt like a complete idiot!

I started back in walking the trail, and about five minutes later, I wound up at the puddle again! Somehow, I had made a complete circle. So, I headed back in, but this time I took a cut-off to the right that I had passed by the first time.

That part of the trail was much more interesting. I came upon a bunch of blackberry bushes, and I really like blackberries! They were ripe for picking at this time of year, so I started munching and couldn't seem to quit. It made me forget all about the stench, just like my lunch had.

I finally pulled myself away from the berries and continued on in search of the Slyfield place. After about twenty minutes of wandering the trail, I didn't seem to be getting any closer to a clearing on the other side of the trees. Now, I was starting to wonder if the Slyfield thing was Leroy's idea of a joke. Travis has mentioned what a strange guy Leroy is, still living with his mama and all.

I had spent enough time on this stink thing, and decided to end my search and get back to work on the barn. I headed back along the trail, but I couldn't resist stopping at the blackberries again. This time when I began picking, it was with the idea of taking home enough to make a pie. I had heard from Travis that the Buettemeier sisters were famous for their pies. I was hoping I could talk them into baking one for me!

TROUBLE COMES TO PALMER LAKE

As I kept picking, I just kept eating. I knew if I continued stuffing my mouth with blackberries, I'd wind up riding the electric toilet just like Anita. Plus, I'd never get my shot at Buettemeier pie!

Just then, I spotted a huge clump of berries way up high. I wasn't sure I could get to them, but I was sure going to try. Those blackberries were too good to pass up, and there must have been a couple hundred in that cluster!

I took the work gloves out of my pocket and put them on, and then positioned myself just right. I jumped up and grabbed for them, but missed. Damn! That cluster was too good to pass up, and I was determined to get it!

I got ready for my second try by running in place for a few seconds. Then I took a deep breath, counted to three, and jumped up as high as I could. This time, I grabbed a hold of them!

Ouch! My arms were scratched and bleeding, and I could barely move! On my way down, I'd lost my footing and fell into the sticker vines! And, I was sure I'd squished the berries! Lying there on my back, I realized that my lust for Buettemeier pie had about done me in!

To make matters worse, the foul smell which was to blame for this whole misadventure was so strong, I began to lose my lunch! I forced myself to roll over on my stomach, even though the stickers pierced my body.

Trapped, and trying to catch my breath, I suddenly began to panic! The source of the foul smell that I'd been searching for was lying in the blackberries beneath me!

Chapter Ten

It was all I could do to get myself unstuck and out of the blackberry vines. Then, I took off running towards the Palmers' house for help, as fast as my scratched and bleeding legs would carry me!

Halfway up the gravel lane, I remembered they were gone. I changed my direction, climbed the fence, and headed for the Lacomes', instead. I knocked on the door and shouted for help, but no one answered. Leroy had already left!

I ran back to the barn, jumped in my truck and floored it, spraying gravel all the way up the lane. I had to go for help, and that meant driving all the way back to Palmer Lake! I ignored the speed limit and kept my foot to the floor, leaving a smoke screen behind and a roar from the muffler like a DC-3 taking off. I passed the Porch Piglet's house doing eighty-five!

Heading into Palmer Lake from the south county area meant Bertha's was the first place I would come to. I slid into the parking lot in a four-wheel drift, then bailed out and ran like my high school girlfriend's father was chasing me. There weren't very many people there yet, but thank god, Travis was at his usual spot!

"Travis, I need your help!"

"Corky, you look like you need a drink. You're as pale as a damn ghost!"

"No time for that right now. We need to go!"

"Corky, get yourself up on that stool and have a cold one."

"Would you just shut up and listen to me for once!"

"Corky, are you setting me up for some kind of a joke?"

That made me mad. I grabbed Travis's drink and poured it on the floor.

"Corky Perkins, are you trying to get yourself killed? That was half a glass of bourbon!"

"Travis, unplug that stool from your ass! We've got to go!"

I grabbed Travis's arm and started pulling, trying to get him off the barstool.

"Corky, now I'm getting pissed! What in the hell do you think you're doing?"

"I'll buy you a double shot later!"

I kept pulling until I got him off his stool, then drug him outside to my truck. I told him to buckle up and hold on tight, then got that old truck burning rubber as we left Bertha's in a cloud of smoke!

"Slow down, Corky! You're going to make me wet my pants!"

"You can take a leak when we get there!"

"Where?"

"The Palmers'."

"You're dragging me all the way out there? Corky, I don't want to spend the rest of the day in the land of manure!"

"Travis, I would welcome a little manure compared to the crap I stumbled into!"

"Don't tell me you and Anita were fooling around in the hay and her husband caught you."

"Would I be dragging you out there if that happened?"

"I don't know. Would you?"

"Travis, don't you ever think about anything besides pork?"

"Yeah, beefcakes, now and then. Hey, your electric toilet didn't burn down the barn, did it?"

"The toilet has nothing to do with it, Travis."

"Well, you made such a fuss over that thing the other night, like you were obsessed or something."

"This is a lot bigger deal than the toilet!"

"Well, thanks to your driving, I'm going to need a few minutes alone with it."

I kept the pedal to the metal all the way out to Corn-Hole County.

"Corky, how much farther is it?"

"Not very. We're almost to the Porch Piglet's house and the turnoff to Thomas Road is just past that."

"You know, Corky, half the time you don't make any sense."

"Travis, right now I don't make any sense to myself!"

"You can say that again. What the hell is a Porch Piglet?"

"See that mailbox coming up? Check out the house and see if the Piglet is out front. Look quick, though, cause I'm not slowing down!"

"You talking about that gal on the sofa?"

"That's her."

"She reminds me of someone I had a few drinks with once."

"Travis, according to you, every woman has spent time drinking in your presence."

"I think her name was Charlene. She showed me how to get back to Palmer Lake after I got lost out here."

"You're always trying to BS me, Travis."

"I'm serious, Corky. Her name was Charlene, but she told me to call her Charlie."

"You sure it wasn't the other way around?"

"What do you mean?"

"That it was actually Charlie, going by the name of Charlene?"

"Real funny."

"Hold on, Travis, here's the turn for Thomas Road."

I was driving so fast, I almost missed the Palmers' driveway!

"Corky, is that their house? It looks like a damn country club!"

"That's it alright, but we're not stopping there. We're heading to the barn."

"Did you ever figure out if Leroy and Mama live next door?"

"They live right over there."

"Whoa! The weeds are up to the windows!"

"Check out Leroy's car collection."

"He sure likes the color rust. They all look the same, except for that black one sticking halfway out of the garage. Mama must have bought him one with paint on it for his birthday!"

I skidded to a stop in front of the barn and we climbed out of the truck. Travis took a couple of steps, then got a funny look on his face.

"Corky, what does that Palmer gal feed her horses? That's the worst manure I've ever smelled!"

"Travis, you can sniff later."

"Hey, where are we going? The barn is this way!"

"Just plug your nose and follow me!"

"Corky, I'm going to bust if I don't take a leak! Where's that potty you're so proud of?"

"I'll show you later. Just come on."

I led the way as we headed for the trail at the

edge of the woods. A few seconds later, I couldn't hear Travis's footsteps behind me, so I turned around. There he stood, starting to sing "Oh My Darling Clementine," while washing away the gravel.

"Corky, I would have preferred to use the toilet, but I guess that's reserved for Anita's fanny."

It took him a couple minutes to do his business, but we finally got to the woods and started walking down the trail. Then we took the path that split off to the right.

"Okay, Travis, I'm going to bring you up to speed."

"It's about time! You drug me off my favorite barstool, and now you're leading me down some skunk path in the woods!"

"Travis, the rotten smell gets worse."

"I thought it was horse manure, but it's way too funky for that."

"Leroy told me the smell was coming from the Slyfield place, on the other side of these woods. After spending time looking, I realized there was no Slyfield place. It was his idea of a joke."

"Leroy thinks he can get away with stuff like that on his home turf, Corky."

"Travis, you see this patch of blackberries? During my Slyfield search, I stopped to sample them. They tasted so good I tried reaching for the biggest cluster I've ever seen. They were up kind of high, so I had to jump. On the way down, I lost my balance and fell right into the middle of the sticker vines."

"Corky, just cut to the chase. That smell is really ripe, and I don't care about no flipping blackberries!"

"Come over here and take a look. This is where I fell."

"I don't care where you fell!"

"Just take a look."

Travis stood there making his famous face of disgust. Then he moved over a few feet and saw it.

"Holy shit, Corky! It's a body! Why didn't you tell me about this?"

"I figured you wouldn't believe me, unless I showed you! You never believe me about anything else!"

"Corky, how long have you known about this?"

"Travis, I went back to town immediately after I discovered it. That's when I found you at Bertha's."

"Did you tell anyone else?"

"No! The Palmers are out of town and Leroy and Mama are at their gas station. I don't know anybody else around here."

"Corky, I apologize."

"Travis, what do you think we should do about this?"

"Well, first, we need to pull the body out of the

sticker bushes so we can get a better look."

"I'm not touching that thing! I already fell on top of it!"

"Corky, it's not going to bite you."

"Travis, there's no way I'm putting my hands on that!"

I turned around to try and get a breath of fresh air. The stench was starting to overpower me again. Then I heard twigs breaking, and when I looked back, Travis was pulling the body out of the blackberries!

"Travis, what are you doing?"

"I'll be a son of a bitch! I don't believe this! Corky, you didn't just find any old body in the bushes. This is Mr. Chicago!"

"Here we go again."

"Corky, I'm serious! I can tell by the fine haircut! And there's that big gold ring on his finger!"

"Are you sure?"

"It's him, all right! Now I know why he didn't come back to get his satchel!"

"Why?"

"Because he was dead!"

"Oh."

"I'm going to see if he's got any ID on him."

Travis started putting his hands in Mr. Chicago's pockets. I don't know how he could stand to do that!

"I'm not finding any ID. The only thing in his pockets is this wad of bills. But I better leave that alone. Hey, look, his shoulder holster is empty!"

"Now what are you doing?"

"I'm going to put him back in the blackberries where he was."

"Why?"

"Because I don't want the cops to know that I've been messing around!"

Travis stuck him back in the bushes, then took a small branch and brushed the dirt around on the trail to get rid of the marks he made.

"Corky, we should get back to town before it gets too late. We've got to figure out how we're going to deal with this."

We left the woods and went back to my truck. When I put the key in the ignition to start it up, Travis grabbed my arm.

"Corky, let's take it easy going back. I'd like to get to Bertha's in one piece. And I'm going to need that double shot you're buying me, after this little adventure."

"I feel like a beer, myself."

We headed for town at a much slower pace than the trip coming out.

"Corky, did I ever tell you about the time I gave a guy a haircut at the mortuary?"

"No way!"

"For real! It was back when I went to barber college. They asked for volunteers, and I was the only one who raised my hand. They even gave me twenty bucks!"

"Travis, you ought to write a book."

"Hey, there's Charlene's place again. Maybe I'll drop in on her, once this dead guy thing is behind us."

"Why do you want to see her?"

"I'm just curious."

"Travis, I don't know how anybody could stand to mess with a dead guy like you did."

"Well, someone had to do it, and I didn't see any volunteers fighting for the privilege!"

"Well, don't look at me!"

"Corky, my Pappy used to tell me it's not the dead ones you need to fear, it's the live ones. Mr. Chicago was one of those guys who bothered me more when he was alive."

"Well, he bothers me more being dead!"

When we finally arrived at Bertha's, I pulled up to the front door, rather than finding a parking spot.

"Corky, are you going in?"

"No, I've changed my mind, Travis. I'd rather go home and hide."

"What about my double shot, and that beer you wanted?"

"Why don't you have a drink for me? Here's a couple bucks."

"Okay, but we need to get together first thing in the morning and tell Sheriff Drew about the body."

"Maybe I'll wake up and find out this whole

thing was a bad dream."

"Not a bad thought. That would take care of the other problem, too."

"What other problem?"

"Anita!"

"Oh, you're right! But wait, if it turns out to be a dream, then I won't have had the experience of installing an electric toilet!"

"You mean the one you found the pile in?"

"Good point."

"Corky, go home and get rested up. I'll meet you in the morning at the barbershop."

Chapter Eleven

As I drove out of the parking lot, Travis stood in front of Bertha's trying to decide what to do. He gave it a moment's thought, then headed inside to his favorite barstool. Bertha sat a double shot in front of him.

Travis needed to sort out all that had transpired over the past few days. He wondered if everything had really happened, or if he was imagining it. After one large swig, everything came clear. It had happened, and he was right in the middle of it!

Rather than dwell on that, he looked around to see if there was anyone at Bertha's that he could shoot the bull with. To his surprise, at the other end of the bar sat Leroy Lacome. Travis couldn't resist walking down and taking the stool next to him.

"Hey, Leroy, how's business over at the gas station?"

TROUBLE COMES TO PALMER LAKE

"'Bout the same as always, Travis."
"How's Mama?"
"'Bout the same as always."
"How's your love life these days, Leroy?"
"None of your business, Travis."

It was always interesting to get the Lacome point of view on things.

"Leroy, I understand that you guys live next door to the Palmers'."

"They moved in next door to us a couple of years ago."

"I'll bet you and Aaron spend a lot of time on his putting green."

"I don't golf."

"Really? Boy, if I had a neighbor with a putting green, I'd be faking it just so I could hang out there."

"Travis, why are you asking about the Palmers?"

"Well, my buddy Corky Perkins is doing some work on their barn. He took me out there today to show off his talents. That's some fancy place they've got there."

"Too big for just two people."

"Leroy, I saw your collection of old gas station signs. They're pretty cool."

"What were you doing at my garage?"

"I wasn't at your garage. I saw them from across the fence when we drove to the barn. Hey, Leroy, what kind of shiny black car is that in there?"

"What are you talking about?"

"We could see the ass end of it sticking out of your garage when we drove by."

"It belongs to one of Mama's friends. I'm putting new spark plugs in it for her. Travis, if Mama was here, she would tell you keep your nose to yourself."

"Hey, Leroy, where are you going? You've still got half a beer left in that bottle."

Travis must have said something that rubbed Leroy the wrong way. Either that, or Leroy was afraid Mama would find out he went drinking.

Travis started looking around to see if there was someone else he could pester, and spotted Birdman and Roland Benton at a table in the back. So, he went over and butted in on their conversation.

Birdman was downing whiskey with a beer chaser. Roland was the lightweight of the group, sipping on a soda. Travis once asked Roland why he didn't care to drink, and his answer was straight to the point, in a roundabout sort of way. Something to do with alcohol not helping or changing nothing, and due to his allergy, it may prove hazardous to other people's health.

The topic of conversation between Roland and the Birdman was an exchange of old war stories about the Marines and the Army Rangers. Travis liked listening to that kind of stuff, especially when told by those two guys. They had earned their bragging rights.

"So, Travis, anything new or interesting

happening to report on?"

"Not a hell of a lot, Birdman. Same old thing, day in, day out."

"Did the mystery man from Chicago ever show up to get his briefcase? We haven't seen anymore of him out at the plant."

"You've got a good memory for a guy who mixes whiskey and beer. But, to answer your question, no, he hasn't returned for it."

"Who the hell are you two talking about?"

"Oh, sorry, Roland. Travis has been asking all around town about a guy he claims left a briefcase at the barbershop, and never came back to get it."

"Birdman, there you go again, trying to put your spin on it."

"You've got to admit, it sounds a little suspicious, Travis."

"Roland, a stranger came in the barbershop a few days ago and got a haircut. When he was done, he grabbed his coat, but forgot his satchel. He still hasn't come back for it."

Travis wasn't about to let on that Mr. Chicago's body was lying in the woods behind the Palmers' barn. He didn't need the Birdman twisting that into one of his distorted tales, making Travis guilty of some kind of foul play. Birdman did that to him once before, when he told people that Travis used to drive an ambulance.

"What did the guy look like, Travis?"

"Well, he was tall, dressed in an expensive suit

and tie, and he was waving a fist full of money at me when he paid for his haircut. He even tipped me ten bucks!"

"That sounds like a guy who was at our place for a massage earlier this week. He was kind of arrogant."

"Roland, did he happen to mention why he was in town?"

"Travis, the guy hardly said a word to me when he came in. Danae had gone to Keselburg for supplies and I was the only one there at the time. When I led him to one of the rooms, he said he didn't want to be touched by a man. I told him that Danae was due back anytime, and he said he'd wait for her. That was the only conversation I had with him."

"Do you know if he said anything to her about why he was here?"

"The only thing Danae mentioned was something about him looking for a gal she'd never heard of."

"The gal's name wouldn't happen to be Sherry Winter, would it?"

"You know, Travis, I don't honestly remember what Danae said her name was. But you're right about the money thing. He gave Danae a fifty-dollar tip!"

Travis felt like he finished the tip race in last place. He polished off his drink, said good-bye, and headed for the door.

Chapter Twelve

Yesterday, when Travis and I returned to Bertha's after checking out the body, I planned on having a drink. But somewhere along the way, I lost my desire. By the time we got there, all I could think about was going home and hiding under the covers.

This morning, I awoke to the sun peeking in my bedroom window around the edges of the blinds. Apparently, I had gotten the sleep I so desperately needed. But now, it was time to get ready and go meet Travis.

As I was heading for the bathroom to take a shower, I happened to notice that my answering machine light was still blinking from a call that came in yesterday. When I got home last night, I just couldn't deal with it.

The message was from Helen Lou Wesson, a spirited old gal who had become a good and trusted friend. I decided to give her a call.

"Corky, I need you to come over and fix my skylights. They were starting to leak last time it rained."

"Helen Lou, I'd be happy to take care of that, but it'll have to wait a few more days. I'm tied up on a barn job."

"A barn job? Nobody in this town has a barn! Are you trying to avoid me?"

"Helen Lou, you're the last person I'd want to avoid. I'm working out of town at Aaron Palmer's place. His wife has horses and I'm fixing up the barn for her."

"I know all about his wife, Corky. She's a slut!"

"Helen Lou!"

"Corky, she's several years younger than he is, and all she wanted was his money. My girlfriends say that she lured him into the bedroom to get it!"

I wasn't about to argue with her, since I had no knowledge of what took place between the sheets at the Palmers'. The little bit that I had spoken with Anita certainly never led me to think of her as a slut!

Now, somewhere in her eighties, Helen Lou Wesson claims to be the oldest living virgin in Palmer Lake. She had her driver's license revoked a couple years ago, but that didn't stop her from taking the old Buick out, and that's actually how we met. I was at the mailbox in front of our local drug store when she drove up and almost hit me. As an apology, she handed me a five-dollar bill.

Helen Lou is a retired Army nurse who spent her career patching up soldiers from WWII and Korea. She had seen her share of dead bodies, so I decided to tell her how my nose led me to finding Mr. Chicago in the woods.

To my surprise, she started to laugh! Somehow, her interpretation was that he died from smelling horse manure! The more serious I tried to be, the worse it got. I finally gave up, and she ended our conversation by telling me how she couldn't wait to tell her friends about it on Sunday.

Palmer Lake doesn't have a church, and except for hardcore bible thumpers Gunther and Ardith McCrumb, local residents just get together on Sunday morning at the Bite Time Café to confess their sins. The McCrumbs drive all the way to Keselburg to attend a real church, then spend the other six days of the week shaking their fingers at the rest of us.

Gunther called me for a plumbing problem last year, and it turned out that a stack of religious books piled on top of their toilet tank was so heavy, it caused a leak in the spud gasket. After fixing the problem, he told me that was a sign for me to start attending church.

I finished my shower and got dressed, then grabbed a piece of toast and hopped in my truck.

When I pulled in the parking lot, I spotted Travis out front on the sidewalk petting the town mutt. As soon as I opened my door, the dog decided it was time to continue on his way. But before he left, he extended his paw and shook hands with Travis, and that earned him a dog biscuit.

"Travis, it looks like you'll always have one friend in town."

"Yeah, he's a good old mutt. He never leaves me wondering or leads me down the wrong road."

"Unlike some of the women you've known?"

"Corky, did you get any sleep last night?"

"Believe it or not, I did. I even had a dream that the Buettemeier sisters made me a pie!"

"I worried about you for a while, after you dropped me off at Bertha's. But I hung out there long enough to get over it."

"You must have had that drink for me, after all."

"And one for me, too."

"Did any strange women show up last night and treat you to a bologna sandwich?"

"No, nothing that exciting. I spotted Leroy Lacome and tried to get a conversation going, but something was bugging him and he split."

"It was probably time for Mama to change his diaper."

"Hey, Corky, I ran into Roland Benton last night, and he told me that Mr. Chicago visited the Rub You Right. He tipped Danae fifty bucks!"

"I wonder what a guy gets from Danae for an extra fifty?"

"You better not let Roland hear you talk that way, or you'll wind up out in the blackberry bushes like someone else we know."

"You didn't tell him about finding the body, did you?"

"No, I'm saving that for Sheriff Ledbutt."

"Speaking of Drew, look who just pulled into the Bite Time parking lot. I guess we won't have to look all over town for him, after all."

"Come on, let's go pay him a visit. Telling him about the dead guy should give him something to chew on besides donuts."

Travis and I walked across the street to the café, and found Sheriff Drew at his usual table. He was just getting started on a bear claw smothered in butter and half a dozen pieces of greasy bacon. With that much fat going in him, I wondered if it oozed out when he got on Danae's massage table?

We sat down next to him, and he immediately started letting everyone in the place know how irritated he was by our presence.

"Sheriff, if you're finished whining and crying, Corky and I need to discuss something with you."

"What could you dumb bastards possibly have to say that would interest me?"

"We've come to see about tickets to the Sheriff's Ball. Oh, wait, that can't be right. Sheriffs don't have any balls!"

"Okay, O'Riley, what's your game?"

"We want to report finding a dead body."

"A dead body? O'Riley, did another one of your girlfriends pass out in the back of your van before you got her pants off?"

"We're serious, Sheriff. Corky found a dead guy at one of his job sites!"

"It's true, Sheriff, I really did!"

"Okay, O'Riley, what's the punch line?"

"There is no punch line. Yesterday afternoon Corky found a body, and he came back to town for help. So, I went with him to have a look. The guy's definitely dead!"

"And he stinks really bad! That's how I found him."

"You two are up to something."

"Sheriff, why don't you stick what's left of that bear claw in your mouth? Then maybe you'll be able to hear what we're trying to tell you!"

"You think you're a regular comedian, don't you, O'Riley? Well, you're about to get yourself locked up for harassment."

"Sounds fun! Do I get my picture in the paper, too?"

"O'Riley, you're walking on thin ice!"

"We wanted to tell you about this last night, Drew, but no one knows where to find you after sunset. Personally, I'm not sure I'd want to know."

"You think you're really going to get me to fall for your bullshit, O'Riley?"

"Sheriff, are you just going to sit here and clog the last of your open arteries, or are you going to get off your ass and investigate?"

I never imagined Travis would talk to the sheriff like that! But it finally lit the fire under Drew, and he shoved what was left of his breakfast aside and grabbed his hat.

"If this turns out to be one of your pranks, O'Riley, I'll have the two of you in my jail. Do you understand me?"

Drew said it loud enough so everyone in the place could hear. Toot happened to be sitting at a table by the front window, and as the sheriff went by, Toot let loose with one. The place broke into laughter.

Out in the parking lot, Drew continued to try and make us believe that he was Super Cop.

"So, Perkins, what kind of help did you think your friend O'Riley would be?"

"Sheriff, I was so frightened by having found this guy, I wanted someone else to verify that he was really dead. I've never been around a dead person before."

"Sheriff, Corky was a basket case. He still is."

"You two get in my car, and we'll go see this so-called dead body."

"Sheriff, how about you and Travis go in your car, and I'll drive my truck. I left all my tools there, and I need to pick them up."

"Perkins, this better not be a practical joke."

"The only joke is seeing Travis in the front seat of a cop car!"

With Drew and Travis riding together, I could only imagine the conversation they would be having!

I arrived at the Palmers' first, and made a bee-line for the barn. I wanted to load up my tools before the action got started. Drew and Travis showed up a minute or two later, and they were arguing.

"Do you really expect me to believe that, O'Riley? First of all, there's no such thing as an electric toilet. And you really think I'm dumb enough to buy into your story about there being a dead body here at Aaron Palmer's estate, of all places?"

"Sheriff, you'll see for yourself."

"You and your buddy Perkins are going to look like twins in those orange jail coveralls."

Then Drew came in the barn and started on me.

"Okay, Perkins, I'm tired of listening to stories about an electric toilet. Let's see this dead guy."

"You need to use the toilet, Sheriff? It's over there in the tack room."

"You two really like to see how far someone will fall for your crap, don't you?"

"Sheriff, I'm not lying! Mrs. Palmer ordered the electric toilet from a catalog!"

"I'm sure Mrs. Palmer has better things to do than order toilets."

"That may be, Sheriff, but then what do you call that?"

"What the hell?"

"Anita left a two-boot load in it, Sheriff."

"Perkins, I want to know where the damn body is!"

I led the way as the three of us walked down the gravel lane, headed for the woods.

"Watch your step, Sheriff. Travis washed away the gravel right there."

"O'Riley did that? That's property damage!"

"I didn't have a quarter on me for the toilet."

"Sheriff, Leroy Lacome sent me on a wild goose chase looking for the Slyfield place. He said that's where the stink was coming from. But after I walked around and didn't find it, I stopped to pick some of these blackberries. That's when I discovered the body."

"You're telling me you found a dead guy in the blackberry bushes?"

"That's right, Sheriff. And he's what was stinking so bad, not the Slyfields' hogs."

"Perkins, then how come I don't smell anything other than blackberries?"

"Well, maybe bodies only stink like that for a little while. What do you think, Travis?"

"I don't know when dead bodies start stinking or when they stop. They sure didn't teach us that in barber college!"

"You two stand back."

Drew pulled his gun and began to move in on the blackberry bushes with all the cunning of an arthritic cougar. After a couple of minutes, he returned.

"I should kick both of you in the ass! Don't you know the difference between a body and an old mattress? I knew this was going to be a waste of time!"

"Sheriff, Corky and I saw the guy laying right there in those very bushes! He was even wearing one of my fine haircuts!"

"O'Riley, how many drinks did you two have before you came out here?"

Travis and I walked over to get a closer look. Sure enough, there in the blackberries was an old mattress rolled up and tied with rope, but no dead guy!

Drew was madder than an old sow bear with a burr in her butt. What worried Travis most was that the sheriff still had a gun in his hand and there were no witnesses in sight!

"I can't believe I came all the way out here just so you two could get your jollies!"

Drew stormed out of the woods and went back to his car. We heard him slam the door, and then he left. Travis and I just stood there looking at each other in disbelief.

"I'm not feeling very good about this, Travis."

"I hear you, Corky. Drew thinks we're a couple of no-good bums with nothing better to do than drag his talcum-powdered ass all the way out here as a joke."

"Travis, did we see a dead body, or didn't we?"

"I didn't drink enough bourbon to make me see an old mattress wearing one of my haircuts!"

"Me, either!"

"Corky, did you see how stupid Drew looked when he pulled his gun? I figured he was going to shoot himself a rabbit for dinner."

We went back to my truck, licking our wounds. We both knew that within hours, Drew would spread the word around town about us. He was famous for that. It seemed like the only thing we could do now was to go to Bertha's and try to restore our confidence.

I fired up the truck and we headed out. When we passed by the Porch Piglet's place, Travis didn't even bother to look. I guess he had other stuff on his mind. Our trip back to town was pretty quiet.

Chapter Thirteen

When we pulled in the parking lot at Bertha's, I spotted the Buettemeier sisters chatting with Billy Hamrod at the front door. Just seeing those girls made me feel better, even if they were hanging out with the town womanizer.

Billy is famous for throwing parties at his house for women only. As the story goes, he always invites an even dozen. It made me wonder if Pinkie and Rosie would stand for playing second fiddle?

Travis and I sat at the bar nursing our second round of drinks, while thinking up names for Drew. Then, Travis brought up the subject of Mr. Chicago's black satchel, and we both decided to screw the sheriff out of his chance to get his hands on it.

"Corky, I think it's time we have a look inside that thing, now that he won't be coming back for it."

"Really? You think that's a good idea?"

"Why not? For all we know, it might just be full of the guy's dirty socks."

"Maybe he was a traveling salesman and his samples are in there."

"Corky, if that guy was a traveling salesman, I'll eat my shorts."

"Better put some mustard on them to go with the mayo."

"Corky, you're sick!"

"You started it!"

"I've noticed that every time you see the Buttmore girls here, you get all clouded in the brain."

"A guy could have worse problems, Travis. Just think about someone like Leroy."

We finished our drinks and headed out to the parking lot. As we started to leave, I noticed the sisters were climbing into Billy's front seat with him, and they were all three laughing. I wondered what was so funny?

When we got to the barbershop, Travis jumped out and had the front door unlocked before I even got the engine shut off.

"Corky, Mr. Chicago's satchel has a lock on it. I'm going to need some tools to get it open with."

"You want me to go get mine out of the truck?"

"No, that wouldn't be any fun. I've got some things around here I think will do the trick."

"So, where is the satchel, anyway?"

"I hid it in the bathroom, behind the senior's toilet paper."

"You still ordering that by the truckload?"

"Twice a year."

"Good thing you don't cut women's hair in here. You'd be ordering it twice a month!"

"Here it is, shiny chrome lock and all. You want to place a bet on what's inside?"

"Nope. I want to see you get the lock open."

"Shouldn't be any big deal. I'll use this paperclip and a drop of clipper oil. Presto, there she is!"

"Travis, how did you do that?"

"It's a family secret. If I told you, I'd have to kill you."

"I've never seen anybody do that before!"

"Corky, in the neighborhood I grew up in, if you couldn't pick a lock by the time you were ten, there was no chance of ever escaping."

"What the heck does that mean?"

"I'll tell you later. Right now, I'm itching to see what's inside this thing."

He opened the satchel and found it crammed full like his wastebasket.

"Travis, what is all that stuff?"

"I don't know, but it sure doesn't look like dirty socks to me."

"I hope there's nothing dead in there."

"Corky, why don't you stick your nose in it and find out. You're an expert on those kinds of things now."

TROUBLE COMES TO PALMER LAKE

"How quickly I forget."

Travis emptied the stuff out on his counter and we started pawing through it.

"Corky, here's some airline tickets, and an envelope from a one-hour photo place."

"Travis, what are all those newspaper clippings?"

"Well, let's see. This is interesting. 'Nicky Torrelli, arrested in connection with Chicago's Westside taxicab robberies.'"

"How about that big one?"

"It says, 'Nicky Torrelli arrested for violating parole.'"

"Are there any pictures?"

"This one's got a picture. And guess who it is?"

"Who?"

"Mr. Chicago!"

"His name is Nicky Torrelli?"

"It was when he was alive."

"Travis, let's check out the envelope from the photo place."

"Here, you take a look while I keep sifting through these articles."

He handed me the red-and-yellow colored envelope, and when I opened it, I could hardly believe my eyes!

"Travis, there's a picture of Anita Palmer in here!"

"Very funny, Corky."

"I'm serious! Her hair is a lot longer, but it's her! Take a look."

"Corky, I don't know what Anita looks like! I've never met her!"

"Travis, I'm going to take a look at those airline tickets."

"Help yourself."

I opened the first one and read the passenger name printed on the ticket.

"Uh, Travis. I think you better see this."

"I'm busy reading these articles."

"Just take a second to check out the name on this one."

"Give it here. Holy crap! Sherry Winter! What's the other one say?"

"Nicholas Torrelli."

Travis and I went through everything in the satchel, and learned that Nicky Torrelli was a small-time mobster in the Chicago area. He had been repeatedly arrested, but was always back on the street a day or two later. They tried to convict him of everything from car theft and illegal gambling to money laundering and dope, but were unable to make it stick.

Sherry Winter had built a rap sheet for herself, as well. There was one article that told about her being busted for pot possession and shoplifting as a minor, but then she moved on to fraudulent check cashing and picking pockets as an adult.

Rounding out the collection of articles was the

one about Torrelli being convicted of running an illegal escort service and getting sentenced to three years in prison. Several women were named in the article, all awaiting their own trials. Sherry Winter was one of them.

"Corky, this article refers to Sherry Winter, as Torrelli's mistress. There's even a picture of her. Here, have a look."

"Travis, that's Anita!"

"Pretty interesting. You think it might have been Torrelli that she was arguing with on the deck that day?"

"I'm starting to wonder. But, Travis, what's with the Sherry Winter name?"

"Well, since you're sure it's Anita in the picture, then it sounds like to me that she changed it. I'll bet she's hiding from the law."

"No way!"

"Corky, at the end of this article, did you happen to read who her attorney was?"

"I only looked at the picture. Why, what's the big deal?"

"It says here, 'Former Chicago attorney, Morgan B. Claymore, will once again represent Miss Winter.'"

"Claymore? Like, Palmer Lake's one and only lawyer? That doesn't make any sense!"

"Corky, I don't know what we've stumbled into, but it's getting more strange by the hour. I'm beginning to think we should do a little snooping around."

"What about the sheriff?"

"Screw the sheriff! Let's play along with his idea of the dead guy in the woods being a practical joke. The less old Ledbutt knows, the better off we'll be."

"Do you think he's going to put us in jail like he said?"

"I don't think he's ever put anyone in jail. If he did, he'd have to stick around to take care of them, and couldn't go fishing."

We continued to read through the stuff for about a half hour more, before calling it a day.

Tomorrow, I was due back at the Palmers' to continue with the barn job, and I needed to get home and rest up. And after reading about Sherry Winter, now I was concerned about Anita, and what she might be capable of if I made her mad!

Chapter Fourteen

The next morning, as I was getting ready to leave, my phone started ringing. Which one of my customers plugged up their toilet this time?

"Good morning, this is Corky."

"Howdy, Corky, this is Toot. I wanted to find out about your date with the sheriff yesterday. He's telling anyone who'll listen what a couple of no-good bums you and Travis are."

"Now, there's a surprise."

"I think he's mad because you guys didn't let him finish up with another helping of bacon grease."

"I liked the send-off you gave him, Toot."

"I'm glad you guys didn't wait any longer to leave. I was about to burst! When I saw you two follow him in, I had Sally change my order to a double cheese omelet just so I'd be sure and have enough ammunition!"

"Toot, have you talked to Travis yet?"

"Not yet. He doesn't have a phone at home, just the one at his shop. But he's not open this early, so I called you first."

"I think you should wait and talk to him about this. The two of you are buddies, and if I spill the beans first, he'd miss out on his chance to shine."

"You're probably right, Corky. He'd get all pissy like a woman if I already knew what he was going to say before he said it."

"Let's not go there!"

"Okay, I'll wait till he opens up. Well, have a good day, Corky. And Corky, remember, don't step in anything I wouldn't!"

"Talk to you later, Toot."

I'd been making progress on the Palmers' barn until the mystery stench turned out to be a dead body. Now, I was guilty of neglecting my duties. The last thing I wanted was to make Anita mad. She might force me to wear her pink rubber boots!

I loaded my tools in the truck and headed out. The pleasant feelings I normally enjoyed during the drive had changed to uneasiness. Finding a dead guy, and then having him disappear, made me squirm.

As I drove past the Porch Piglet's house, I spotted her on the sofa, puffing and brushing. I decided it might be neighborly to stop by and meet her, since Travis thought he recognized her. So, I hung a u-turn.

There wasn't a driveway at her place, just a

bunch of tire tracks in the dirt. So, I pulled up to the porch and got out.

"Hey, hotrod! What the hell do you think you're doing? You can't just drive across my yard!"

"You wouldn't happen to be Charlene, would you?"

"I'm your worst nightmare, lead foot!"

"I'll bet your friends call you Charlie."

"How do you know my name?"

"A guy by the name of Travis told me."

"Travis? I don't know any Travis! Say, what are you trying to pull? I've got a shotgun right here, and I'm about to point it in your direction!"

"Travis said it's been a couple of years since he picked you up hitching. You showed him the way back to Palmer Lake."

"Palmer Lake? I don't go to Palmer Lake! Nothing ever happens there."

"That's a fact, Charlie."

"Hey, I don't like you calling me Charlie!"

"Okay, Charlene. Anyhow, Travis said that when the two of you got to town, you went to Pop's Saloon for a drink. Ring a bell?"

"Are you talking about the guy with the van that had the bitchin' stereo? You say his name is Travis? I'm not much good at remembering names."

"Travis and I are best friends, except when I beat him at checkers."

"Checkers? That's a game for old men who fart a lot!"

"If you only knew."

"He put you up to this?"

"In a manner of speaking. I've been working on one of your neighbor's barns, and Travis rode out with me to see the place. He noticed you on the porch when we drove by and thought you looked familiar. I decided to stop and find out, so he can quit wondering."

"Does he still have his van?"

"Yeah, but most of the time he rides a motorcycle."

"He's got a motorcycle, too?"

"Sure does."

"Is he married?"

"Not legally."

"Is he still a barber in Palmer Lake?"

"The one and only."

"Whose barn are you working on?"

"Some folks by the name of Palmer."

"Anita Palmer's place?"

"Yeah, do you know her?"

"Everyone around here knows who she is. She's got the idea that she's too good for us local yokels."

"Maybe it's all an act."

"She does a real good job of acting, then."

"Charlene, I think she's just trying to make people believe she's someone she's not."

"It's called, 'thinking your shit don't stink!'"

"You call em like you see em, don't you, Charlene?"

"So, you work on barns, huh?"

"Well, this is my first one. I usually work on houses."

"You know anything about fixing toilets?"

"No, I avoid those things. They scare me!"

"That's too bad."

"Why? Do you have potty problems?"

"What did you say your name was?"

"Corky Perkins."

"Well, Corky Perkins, you don't go asking a lady if she's got potty problems. That's personal!"

"You know what I meant, Char."

"Just fooling with you, Cork. So, how do I get word to Travis, anyhow?"

"What would you like to say?"

"How about telling him to stop by and see me after work. I'll fix him supper."

"I'll pass that along, Charlie. I'm sure he'll get all excited when he finds out it was you he saw on the porch."

"Hey, watch your mouth!"

"Now what?"

"Just kidding! Tell Travis to bring the music with him that we listened to in his van."

"Well, I've got to get to the barn, but I'll be sure and tell Travis it really was you that he saw on the porch. See you later, Charlene."

"Corky, it's Charlie to you."

I pulled out of her yard and continued on towards the Palmers'. It only took a couple of minutes before I came to their driveway and started down the gravel lane. Then, out of nowhere, a thought hit me. Would I run into the dead guy again, and find him in a horse stall or the hayloft this time? It was giving me the creeps!

I parked at the barn and was about to unload my tools when I changed my mind. I wanted to check and see if the dead guy was here first. But just then, I heard a familiar voice.

"Why isn't the barn finished? How long is this going to take? The lights aren't all up, and the window isn't even in! And there's no door on the tack room! I knew I shouldn't have gone out of town!"

She was back, and she was in true form. It was that friendly, welcoming voice, missing for the past few days. Anita!

"Good morning, Mrs. Palmer."

"What's so good about it, Corky? I figured when I got back, everything would be done. But I can't even use the toilet, without the door!"

"Well, the missing door didn't stop someone from using the toilet earlier, did it?"

"What are you talking about?"

"Anita, when I came to work the other morning, prepared to finish wiring the toilet, I was greeted by some surprises."

"Surprises? What kind of surprises?"

"Somebody screwed around with the wiring. They tried to hook it up themselves so they could incinerate a rather large load. I had to correct the faulty wiring, and then remove the pile, before I could make any progress."

"I have no idea what you're talking about. Anyhow, that certainly couldn't have delayed you for more than an hour or so. I don't understand why you still have so much left to do!"

"There were some things that I needed your okay on before I continued, but you were gone."

"Corky, you had my authorization to do whatever was necessary!"

Funny how I didn't remember hearing that from her in any of our conversations. It looked like there was just no winning this war of words, so I decided it was time to pull out the ace.

"The only authorization I got came from Nicky Torrelli."

That did the trick! Anita looked like she was going to pass out. She stumbled over to the wooden bench next to the barn door and sat down. For once, she was speechless! Of course, that only lasted for a few seconds.

"How do you know his name?"

"Oh, a little bird told me."

"What else do you know about him?"

"I know that you were arguing with him on your deck a few days ago."

"Where were you?"

"I was here at the barn working. Then I heard you screaming, and that's when I saw you run him off."

"What did you hear?"

"I couldn't tell what you were saying, if that's what you mean."

"Nothing?"

"Just screaming and yelling as you chased the guy around the side of your house."

"He really made me mad!"

"So, where have you been the past few days?"

"Aaron surprised me with a trip to Canada. He likes to go golfing there, and I like to spend time at the vending machines in the hotel."

"Sounds fun."

"Well, it's nice to visit a big city again. Living out here, I forget what people look like."

"Nicky came by while you were gone."

Anita's eyes got great big and she looked like she was going to get sick. Already kind of pasty-skinned, anyway, she appeared almost ghostly when I said that.

"So, who is this Torrelli character, anyhow?"

"He was my boyfriend, when I lived in Chicago."

"What brings him to our part of the world?"

"He showed up without warning, looking for me. That's what caused the argument you saw on the deck."

I wasn't ready to tell Anita that I found Nicky's body in the woods, and I could tell that she wasn't letting me know any more than she was comfortable with, either. She did seem to have forgotten her hostilities about the barn not being finished, though.

She slowly got up from the bench and tried taking a few steps. She was still pretty weak, but went ahead and started walking towards the house. I waited to see if she would start a conversation with her invisible friend, but she didn't. I must have really touched a nerve.

I got back to work on the barn, and finished up late in the afternoon, finally completing all the items on her list. Then I loaded up my tools, got in the truck, and headed out.

As I passed by the Porch Piglet's place, I didn't see her out front, but I went ahead and honked, anyway. I figured she was probably inside taking a nap, worn out from brushing her golden locks. I wonder what Travis thinks of hair like that? I'll have to ask, when I tell him about meeting her.

Chapter Fifteen

While I spent my day banging heads with Anita, Travis's day started off with a bang, as well. The closer gizmo on the front door of the barbershop broke, and the door slammed shut, pinching his ass!

The door breaking really pissed him off, but that took second place to his other concerns. Travis couldn't seem to get his mind off of the contents of Mr. Chicago's satchel, making it hard for him to think about cutting hair. He felt like he should be on the radio or TV, telling everyone about the secret identity of Anita Palmer.

His thoughts about being a news announcer were interrupted by his first customer of the day, Loren Yates. Loren owns the Legend Motel, here in Palmer Lake.

"Hey, Loren. How's fishing season treating you?"

"We're full up, Travis."

Loren is the second generation of Yates to operate the motel, and he has made several changes since taking control. During fishing seasons of years gone by, the place would attract the usual handful of regulars. But ever since he started offering movie rentals, now when fishing season starts, the place is full to capacity.

"Anything new this season to offer the fishermen?"

"Well, as a matter of fact, yes. I've decided to have Saturday evening barbeques."

"What's up with that?"

"The guys can get together for eats, and share fishing tips."

"When do you plan to start that?"

"I already did. This past Saturday was the first one."

"Was there much of a turnout?"

"We went through thirty pounds of hamburger and chicken, along with twenty pounds of bean salad."

"That must have made for a noisy crowd. Did you learn any new secrets?"

"You know, I did, but they didn't have anything to do with fishing."

"You lost me there, Loren."

"Travis, most of the conversations I overheard were about the movie rentals I offer. Seems several of the guys were disappointed that I didn't have certain titles available."

"What movies were they asking for?"

"The one I heard mentioned again and again was called, 'The Lure of Lori.'"

"Oh yeah, that's a good one."

"You've seen it, too?"

"Well, now wait. What did you call it?"

"The Lure of Lori."

"No, I was mistaken. I was thinking about a mud-wrestling flick I saw, with a naked midget gal. I think it was called, 'The Horror of Midgie.'"

"Travis, have you been getting enough sleep? You seem confused."

"I've had a lot on my mind lately."

"Why? What's going on?"

"Loren, you didn't happen to have a guy from out of town staying at the motel, did you?"

"Travis, don't be ridiculous. All our guests are from out of town. Who'd you have in mind?"

"The guy I'm talking about is from Chicago, and he didn't come for the fishing."

"Oh, him. I couldn't forget that guy! He acted real cool, like he was trying to impress me, or something. He even paid for a week's stay in advance, with cash."

"Did you happen to notice what kind of vehicle he was driving?"

"It was an older, nice-looking black Caddy, with Diamond Car Rental license frames. Next to all the pickup trucks in my parking lot, his car stood out like a naked lady at a bus stop!"

"By any chance was his name Nicky Torrelli?"

"That's the guy. Quite the character, wouldn't you say?"

"Yeah, he stopped in here for a haircut, and just like you said, he played it real cool. He even tipped me ten bucks."

"That's a week's pay for you!"

"When's the last time you saw him, Loren?"

"The only time I ever saw him was when he first checked in. His week was up a couple days ago, but he never checked out, or turned in his key. When I went looking for him, I got no answer at the door, so I used my master key and went in, and found the room empty."

"What do you do in a situation like that?"

"I had no choice but to change the lock. Travis, why do you care about him, of all people?"

"He left his satchel here, and he's never come back to get it."

"Well, if it was me, I'd just turn it over to the sheriff and let him worry about it. Then you don't have to."

"I've been told that before."

"Travis, I've got to get back to the motel. Thanks for the trim."

"Hope you get your key back."

The rest of the day was the usual run of old men, stopping by to see if Travis was still breathing. Toot showed up to ask about our visit with Sheriff Drew, and mentioned that we were rapidly becoming the talk of the town. Travis had to play down the truth, cause he didn't want it getting around that we were involved with a missing dead guy.

At the end of the day, Travis decided to head over to Bertha's. Before he left, he grabbed a couple of the newspaper articles about Nicky and Sherry so he could reread them.

As he was locking the door, he happened to meet up with Mary Ellen Smythe on the sidewalk. As always, she was wearing one of her sweet smiles.

"Good evening, Ms. Smythe. How are you doing?"

"I'm doing fine, Travis. It's nice to see you."

"Where are you headed this fine evening?"

"I have a couple of errands to do, and I decided to walk instead of drive, since it's so nice out. What about you?"

"I'm headed to Bertha's."

"What a coincidence. I was just thinking about stopping by there myself, after I finish my errands."

"Well, then, how about I buy you a drink?"

"That sounds great. I'll see you there, after a bit."

Travis climbed on his motorcycle and headed out. The evening air was warm, and the bugs were all fighting for a place in his teeth.

When he got to Bertha's, he spotted Attorney

TROUBLE COMES TO PALMER LAKE

Claymore sitting at the bar. That was almost too good to be true. Claymore was someone Travis really wanted to talk to, now that he'd read his name in the Sherry Winter articles. So, he sat down next to him and began a friendly conversation.

"Buy me a drink, sailor?"

"Only if you're having bourbon."

"So, you're a mind reader now."

"How are you doing, Travis?"

"Well, now that you've asked, I guess I'll have to tell the truth."

"That would be a first!"

"M.B., I want to know all about Aaron and Anita Palmer."

"What's to tell?"

"My friend Corky Perkins has been working on their barn. He talks a lot about Anita, and I was wondering how she and Aaron met. I've always heard that she isn't from around here."

"Travis O'Riley, since when are you interested in romance? One-nighters in the back of your van is how you spell love."

"Don't knock it, if you haven't tried it!"

"Travis, did that stranger ever come back and pick up his briefcase? You were all worried about it last time we talked."

"Well, let me spell it out for you, M.B."

"Please do."

"Corky spotted Anita Palmer having a heated discussion with some guy on her deck the other day. He was tall, and dressed in a suit and tie, just like the guy who left the satchel at my place."

"I'm confused, Travis."

"Word on the street is, Anita came from Chicago, same as you."

"Bertha, I'd like another drink! Make this one a double, and bring Travis one, as well."

"That's white of you, M.B."

"Travis, how about we trade stories. I'll tell you what I know, and you tell me what you know. We'll just keep it to ourselves, and no one will be the wiser."

"Sounds fair. How about you go first."

"Well, Aaron Palmer and I made a few trips to Chicago for his company's business. Since I'd had my law practice there for thirty years, he asked me to be his advisor. Anita was the daughter of a close friend of mine, and I had the opportunity to introduce Aaron to her on one of those trips."

"Sounds a little too innocent, if you ask me."

"That's how it happened, Travis. Love at first sight."

"Let's cut the crap, M.B. I happen to know that you represented Anita when she was in trouble with the law."

"Where do you get your information, Travis?"

"You ever heard of the newspapers?"

"They like to sensationalize the facts to sell more copies."

"Let me run shoplifting and pot possession as

a minor by you."

"What else do you think you know?"

"I know there's a lot more to Anita than anyone in Palmer Lake could imagine. Like Sherry Winter, for example."

"Okay, Travis, let's quit playing cat and mouse. You obviously know more than you should, so why don't you tell me what's going on."

"M.B., when you were in for your haircut, I told you about the guy leaving his satchel. You knew it was Nicky Torrelli from the get-go!"

"I don't know what you're talking about."

"I figured you'd say that. Here, take a look at these newspaper articles."

Claymore's face turned to marshmallow as he recognized the two clippings from the Chicago paper. Travis wasn't aware the small-town lawyer had such a big appetite for bourbon. He was rapidly drinking Travis under the table.

"Travis, you know too much for your own good. This could land you in a real mess."

"M.B., I've been in messes all my life. This is just another notch on my belt. I think you were looking out for your friend's daughter, and you stepped in something bigger than you could scrape off your shoe."

"Her father told me her problems were always minor. But the older she got, the bolder she got. When Sherry fell in with Torrelli and his organization, I knew it was only a matter of time before she would wind up behind bars. Her father was terminal, and after his passing, I felt I had to do something to help her. That was during the time that Aaron and I took our first trip to Chicago."

"How did you get them together?"

"I showed Aaron a picture of Sherry. He said she was attractive and thought it would be interesting to meet her. That same week, Torrelli was convicted for his illegal escort activity, and Sherry was one of several girls who were connected to him."

"This is starting to sound pretty good, M.B. It'd be my guess that you turned to your friend Aaron Palmer, because of his money and influence."

"Well, Travis, that is exactly what I did. Seeing that Aaron was attracted to her, I worked out an arrangement with him."

"What about Sherry's court date?"

"The judge overseeing all of this Torrelli escort business was a long-time friend. I met with him in his quarters and explained how Sherry had been led down the wrong path. I told him that arrangements could be made that would allow Sherry to start her life over, with Aaron as her guardian. The judge thought it would be good to get her away from Chicago, so he took care of all the details."

"M.B., this sounds more like a movie than real life."

"It's all in who you know, Travis."

"So, where did the name 'Anita' come from?

Her real name is Sherry."

"Anita is her middle name. Sherry Anita Winter."

"I knew it!"

"Knew what?"

"Oh, nothing."

"Travis, we'll keep this between us, right?"

"You can take it to the bank, M.B."

"The drinks are on me tonight, Travis. Here's a couple of twenties. Make sure Bertha gets them. I've got things to go take care of."

Claymore cut Travis off before he could ask him any more questions about Sherry and Nicky. But Travis was starting to get red and sweaty. His excitement glands smelled trouble.

As Claymore headed for the door, it was obvious the attorney had one too many double bourbons under his belt. He slipped on the vinyl floor, grabbing onto the door handle just in the nick of time. Travis thought for sure he was going down.

At the same time Claymore was heading out, Mary Ellen Smythe was heading in. She backed away from the door to give him plenty of room. The look on her face as he tried to steady himself was pretty funny. Travis got up from his barstool to greet her.

"Hey, Mary Ellen, did you finish running your errands?"

"Travis, did you see that? Attorney Claymore is shit-faced! Excuse me, I mean intoxicated."

"You don't say?"

"I do say! He can barely walk! Somebody should take him home and put him to bed before he hurts himself."

"Are you volunteering?"

"Don't be ridiculous, Travis. My schedule doesn't include taking care of old men."

"Let's grab us a table, Mary Ellen, while the night's still young."

The waitress was a new face. She had flaming red hair and a nametag that read, 'Pepper.' Mary Ellen ordered a Pink Squirrel, with a double shot of tequila. Travis kept an eye on Pepper as she headed back to the bar.

"Travis O'Riley, get your mind out of the gutter! She's way too young for you!"

"I was just admiring her long, red hair. I don't ever get to see hair like that in my barbershop."

"Good comeback, Travis, but you're only fooling yourself."

"I guess I couldn't help it. Old habits die hard."

"You'll be dying hard, alright, if you keep sniffing around young girls."

"Mary Ellen, regarding your choice of spirits - is it the tequila or the Pink Squirrel that acts as the chaser?"

"Does it matter?"

"Well, I was just curious. I've never heard of that combination before."

"Travis, you try working for Mayor Frederick P. Bartholomew, and see if your drinking habit doesn't pick up speed. He was in his office the entire day today. What a pain in the rear."

"Sounds like you had a tough time."

"So, tell me, Travis, how was your day?"

"It was quite productive, actually. I cut several heads today and had an interesting visit with Loren Yates."

"How is Loren? I haven't talked to him for a long time."

"He says that the motel is filled up for fishing season. Apparently he's done some things that have made the place more popular, like offering movie rentals and holding barbeques."

"I've heard about his disgusting movies."

"Oh, Mary Ellen, but how bad can a fishing video be?"

"More like fishing in all the wrong places, Travis."

"I had an uncle who got in trouble for fishing in the wrong place once. He cast his line in the neighbor's wife's pond."

"Must be a family tradition. Did you and Loren talk about anything besides his movies?"

"Well, yes. He and I have something, or I should say someone in common."

"Don't tell me you both went fishing in the same pond as your uncle?"

"No, nothing like that, Mary Ellen."

"Well, what then?"

"A few days ago, I had a customer who left his satchel at the barbershop, and he's never returned to get it."

"What's that got to do with Loren Yates?"

"Turns out the guy was staying at the motel. He registered for a week's stay, but never checked out, or returned the room key at the end of the week."

"There's never a shortage of irresponsible people out there, Travis. We just saw one trying to leave here a few minutes ago."

"Claymore?"

"Travis, you seem a little befuddled. Is there something you're not telling me?"

"My buddy Corky has been working at Aaron Palmer's place, on their barn. He saw this same guy having an argument with Anita Palmer. Then I heard from Birdman that the guy was causing trouble out at Palmer Industries."

"Sounds like a real jerk."

"The guy is from Chicago, and he's got an attitude problem."

"Oh, my, look at the time! I didn't realize it was so late! I hate to be rude, Travis, but I'm supposed to meet a friend this evening. Since I'm walking, I better be on my way."

"But don't you want to hear the best part?"

"I do, but unfortunately it will have to wait. I'll see you later, Travis. Thank you for the drink."

TROUBLE COMES TO PALMER LAKE

Mary Ellen hightailed it out of there, like she'd placed too much confidence in a fart.

"Pepper, I need another shot!"

This was just one more reason that Travis preferred his van-girls. They always stayed for the best part! One gal, on her second visit, even brought a ruler with her. In the end, though, it turned out that she's the one Travis wanted to hide from when he relocated to Palmer Lake.

Chapter Sixteen

My drive back and forth to the Palmers' really burned up the fuel, and when I got back to town, I was running on empty again. I've thought about buying a newer truck that gets better gas mileage, but I'm emotionally attached to my old rust-bucket. With the canopy on back, it became my private love-nest after I got old enough to drink. But that's another story.

I needed to head to the one-and-only gas pump in town, the Lacomes' service station, and I was hoping to make it there before they closed. Their hours of operation tend to fluctuate as evening draws near, based on what Mama Lacome finds to watch on TV.

When I reached the station, the lights were still on, so I pulled up to the pump and parked.

As much as I hated to use their restroom, I really had to go. There was a motorcycle parked by the door, so I figured I'd have to wait. But being desperate, I knocked, and then tried the knob. The door was unlocked.

When I switched on the light, I went into shock! All four bulbs in the light fixture were working, and the restroom was spotless! Even the smell of dead hamster was gone! Somebody had spent some serious time cleaning! The phone numbers and messages were gone from the walls, and I didn't even stick to the seat this time!

When I returned to my truck, out from the office came a skinny gal with long black hair.

"Fill it up with regular, mister?"

"Uh, yeah."

My thoughts were instantly transformed from the subject of gasoline to unmentionables. I watched her fill my tank, wash the windshield, check the oil, and even check the air pressure in all four tires. Then it hit me - she must be responsible for the clean restroom!

When she was all done, I followed her back inside to settle up. As she reached over the counter to hand Mama the slip of paper with my total on it, I noticed her arm was covered with tattoos. Then she headed back outside to help another customer.

"So, Mama, who's the new helper?"

"That's Lorraine."

"I've never seen her around here before. What's the deal?"

"Leroy needed a little time off, so we hired her."

"She sure seems to know what she's doing. I was impressed by the clean restroom."

"That girl has a need to clean everything in her path, Corky. She even got rid of the dead squirrel from the side of the road."

"Leroy must need the time off, because he's taking work home with him now."

"Taking work home with him? That's a good one!"

"He told me he was working on your friend's car there."

"What in the world are you talking about, Corky?"

"I saw a black car sticking out of your garage the other day, when I was at the Palmers'. I talked to Leroy, and he told me he was doing your friend a favor, changing the spark plugs."

"I don't know anything about any favors, Corky. Leroy's been taking time off to go bowling."

"Bowling?"

"He and his buddy are practicing. There's a tournament coming up at Keselburg Lanes that pays five hundred to the winner, plus a year's free bowling."

"I didn't know he was into that. Does Leroy have his own ball?"

"He's got two. He was born with them."

That was the first time I'd ever heard a joke

from Mama Lacome! What made it even funnier - Leroy was the last guy you'd think had balls!

I wondered whose car was in their garage, then? It was there for two or three days. How could Mama miss seeing it? This was starting to sound like a bad case of gutter balls to me!

"Mama, whose motorcycle is that, parked by the restroom?"

"That belongs to Lorraine."

"She rides a motorcycle?"

"Pretty foolish, if you ask me."

"She seems like a very interesting girl."

"Cool down, big boy. Lorraine's already got a partner. They live together in one of Chuck Schmeer's rental houses."

"Just my luck."

"Don't go losing any sleep over her, Corky. This is a big world, with lots of real women in it."

"Real women?"

"That's what I said. Real women."

"I'll try to remember that. Thanks for the gas, Mama."

I went back out to my truck and spotted Lorraine, bending over to check the air in the other customer's tire. Her shirt was pulled up in back, exposing another tattoo. I don't know what Mama meant, but Lorraine sure looked real to me!

I left the station and headed for Bertha's, eager to meet up with Travis. When I pulled in the parking lot, I spotted the Buettemeier sisters with

Billy Hamrod again. The guy must have a natural gift that women find irresistible. Either that, or it was his white Panama hat. I wonder if he'd let me borrow it? Maybe then Lorraine would find me irresistible!

When I went inside, Travis wasn't on his barstool, so I figured he must be in the head. As I stood there waiting for him, I spotted something that made me do a double take. Travis was sitting alone at a table!

"Travis, what are you doing over there? Your barstool is getting jealous!"

"Oh, no big deal. I was having a drink with Mary Ellen Smythe."

"Am I interrupting?"

"No, Mary Ellen had to go meet someone. You want a drink?"

"That sounds like a good idea."

"I'll flag down the new waitress. Her name's Pepper."

"Pecker? What kind of a name is that for a waitress?"

"No, you idiot, Pepper. Like salt and pepper. Look, here she comes."

"Ooh, nice hair! Ooh, nice body, too!"

"What can I get for you boys?"

"I'll have another bourbon, and Corky wants a beer."

"I'll be right back with your order."

"So, Corky, what do you think? Is she a hot

little number, or what?"

"She certainly is! But what about Lindsey?"

"I haven't seen her around tonight. Anyhow, I'm swearing off Lindsey."

"Looking at Pepper, I'd say she's way too young for you, as well, Travis. Don't you think you better set your sights on someone a bit older?"

"Who do you know around here that could compare to Pepper or Lindsey?"

"I'm not talking about comparing. I'm talking about someone who wants you to come to dinner."

"Corky, does your truck have an exhaust leak? You're sounding way out there, as usual."

"Travis, Charlene wants to see you again."

"Alright, what's the joke?"

"I'm serious! I stopped by the Porch Piglet's place to see if she was the gal you thought she was, and sure enough, it's her! She even told me that she remembered your van, and what a great stereo you had in it. She wants you to come to dinner at her place, and to be sure and bring the music."

"Corky, quit it."

"Travis, you think whatever you want, but the Piglet is hot for you. I think she's planning on serving you marinated tube steak!"

"You really stopped there?"

"She gave me a hard time at first, but once I told her I knew the barber who picked her up a few years ago, she changed her tune. She even insisted that I call her Charlie."

"What else did she have to say?"

"Well, we didn't visit very long, but one thing that seemed to excite her was your motorcycle."

"You told her about that?"

"She lit up like a road flare, Travis. If I were you, I'd hop on that bike and get out there."

"You sure you're not just spinning another one of your tales?"

"No monkey doo-doo, this time."

"I'll have to give this some thought."

"Hey, Travis, wait till you hear about my conversation with Anita Palmer."

"You saw her, too?"

"Yep. She showed up this morning and started right in giving me lip about the barn not being finished. So, I decided to see what her reaction would be if I mentioned Nicky Torrelli."

"You didn't tell her he's dead, did you?"

"No. I told her that he came by while they were gone."

"What did she say to that?"

"She kind of went into a trance, and actually told me that he used to be her boyfriend."

"No kidding?"

"I could sense that she was covering for him, though. She headed back to the house, barely able to walk. Mentioning his name really had an effect on her."

"Corky, this thing is getting even more

mysterious. I had a visit today from Loren Yates, and he told me that Torrelli was registered at the motel. He said that Nicky Boy disappeared and never turned in his key."

"Really?"

"He also said that Torrelli was driving an older black Caddy, with Diamond license frames."

"Travis, I stopped by the Lacomes' station on my way here, to fill up. When I mentioned to Mama the black car that Leroy was working on at home, she gave me a ration of crap. She claims that he never worked on any black car at home!"

"Corky, something's going on."

"That's not all. There's a girl pumping gas at their station now. Mama said that Leroy is taking time off to go bowling!"

"Bowling? I smell a floater in the punchbowl, Corky."

"Travis, the more I think about it, bowling does kind of fit with Leroy's ambition in life."

"You've got a point there. But Leroy never takes time off."

"The gal pumping gas is hot! She rides a motorcycle, and she's covered in tattoos!"

"Corky, since when are you interested in a girl like that?"

"Don't worry, Mama says she's already got a boyfriend."

"When has that ever stopped you?"

"Maybe I'll just see where things lead."

"I'm sure you will."

"Travis, what do you think we should do about Torrelli now that he's among the missing?"

"I've been thinking about that. Corky, are you heading to Keselburg anytime soon?"

"I'm going to Jumbo's Hardware tomorrow. Why?"

"I think we need to find out if that black Caddy is back at Diamond Car Rentals or not. You up for that?"

"You want me play private investigator? Cool!"

"Calm down, Corky. We don't want anyone figuring out what we're up to. Why don't you make up some story about how you like the older cars they rent, and flow with that."

"That's a great idea!"

"Well, my bunions are throbbing. I'm ready to call it a night."

"I hear Charlene's an expert on throbbing. Go see her, Travis. You'll be calling the shots."

"I always do."

Chapter Seventeen

The next morning, I was all revved up about heading to Diamond Car Rentals to see what I could find out about the black Caddy. I also had to pick up my supplies at Jumbo's Hardware. The men's room at Jumbo's has seven stalls, and that was reason enough to make the trip!

As I was getting ready for my journey, the phone rang. It was Helen Lou Wesson again, wanting to know how come I hadn't fixed her skylights yet. I tried to think up something brilliant to say, other than I was busy, but my imagination was exhausted.

"Helen Lou, it's always good to hear your voice."

"Corky, don't start. Is someone else paying you more than I do?"

"That's not a very nice thing to say. I've just been behind the eight ball with that big job out at the Palmer place."

"Corky, when I go play cards with the girls on Wednesday, sometimes the Palmers are our main topic of conversation."

"Really? What do you girls find so interesting about them?"

"We like to talk about what a floozy Mrs. Palmer is."

"Helen Lou, maybe there's really a romance between them."

"Betty Jossington dated Aaron Palmer before he got married. She claims their fling ended because he was impotent."

"Who's Betty Jossington?"

"She's one of our former teammates."

"Well, if he's impotent, Helen Lou, how could Anita have lured him into the bedroom for his money?"

"Betty liked to brag about her romances. We all wondered why she even cared about doing it with him, since prune juice is all that really matters at our age."

"What became of old Betty?"

"She moved to Texas, to look for a cowboy with a big saddle horn."

"Helen Lou!"

"Don't forget about my skylights, Corky. I've got some leftover tuna fish in the icebox, so I'll fix you lunch."

"Okay. I'll get there as soon as I can."

I finished getting ready, then fired up my truck

TROUBLE COMES TO PALMER LAKE

and headed out. I started thinking about how outrageous it would be to run into Lorraine at Jumbo's! A chick that rode a motorcycle was bound to visit a hardware store for a screw now and then.

When I arrived, I decided to do some looking around first, and wound up finding a new drill bit sharpener, along with the toilet parts I came to get. The tool department had made me forget all about Lorraine, but when I visited the men's room, I had visions of her tattoos.

Diamond Car Rentals was just a mile down the road, and their huge sign was all lit up like a Christmas tree. When I pulled in, I expected to see Little Detroit, but there were only about a dozen cars, and the office was a singlewide trailer.

I went inside, and was instantly overpowered by the smell of hot butter. In the corner was one of those circus wagon popcorn machines. It was all lit up, as well. The guy behind the counter was munching away.

"Good morning. May I help you?"

"I hope so. I'm interested in finding out about your older rental cars."

"I'm Byron Blazer, the owner, but you can call me Carrot."

"Carrot?"

"That's right. All my friends have been calling me that since grade school. It's because of my orange hair."

"What's with the popcorn machine?"

"Want some? There's always plenty of corn here at Diamond Car Rentals. Just help yourself."

"Where did you ever find a machine like that?"

"Uncle Ernie picked that up for me in Mexico."

As I was scooping up a bag, I glanced out the window. There, on the back lot behind the office, sat an older black Cadillac.

"Carrot, this tastes pretty good."

"It's our secret recipe. Keeps people coming back."

"I'm not currently in the market for a rental, but I would appreciate some information."

"What kind of information?"

"I'm trying to find out about an older, black Cadillac. It was spotted in Palmer Lake recently, and it had Diamond license frames on it."

"We've only got one Caddy in our fleet."

"Is that it out back? I noticed it through the window."

"That would be it."

I pulled out the newspaper article that had Torrelli's picture in it and showed it to Carrot.

"Would you happen to know if this is the guy who rented it?"

"That's him, alright. Can't forget a guy like that."

"How so?"

"Well, his name, for one thing. Sounded like a

pizza place. Then there was the way he acted, like he thought he was better than other people."

"Did he cause you any trouble?"

"Not really, but I sure felt uncomfortable around him. He was dressed real fancy, and he paid me up front in cash. No one rents a car with cash."

"When did he return the car?"

"He didn't. Some other guy brought it back. He said Torrelli had to leave town unexpectedly and he was returning it for him."

"What was that guy's name?"

"That's the strange part. Since the car came back early, and Torrelli had paid cash in advance, he was due a partial refund. I wanted to give the guy back the money, but he wouldn't show me any ID."

"What did this guy look like?"

"He was kind of pudgy and dirty, and he had on a old bowling shirt covered with grease. He handed me the keys, then headed out the door and hopped on the back of a waiting motorcycle, and off they went."

"Was the car okay?"

"Yeah, it seems to be fine. It kind of stinks, though."

"Did you get a look at the driver of the motorcycle?"

"With the helmet on, I couldn't see the driver's face, but both arms were covered with tattoos."

"I see a lot of bikers with tattoos. That's pretty common."

"I suppose."

"Well, listen, Carrot, thanks for the info on the Caddy. And thanks for the popcorn. It's really good!"

"Are you a private detective?"

"Not quite yet. I still have a few more lessons to complete from the correspondence school."

"Do you have a business card?"

"No, they won't let us get cards made until we finish the course."

"Well, after you graduate, come see us if you need to rent a car for undercover work."

"Will do. Thanks again, Carrot."

On my way out, I stuck my head around the corner of the office and got a better look at the black Caddy. The lot boy was busy washing the windows, and when he saw me eyeballing him, he stopped what he was doing.

"Hey, dude. Pretty nice rod, wouldn't you say?"

"It sure is. You work here?"

"Duh."

"What's your name?"

"I'm Jimmy."

"Well, Jimmy, it looks like you're getting it all cleaned up and ready to rent."

"It's going to have to sit for a couple days. It smells like old gas inside, so we've got to let it air out."

"I'll bet you run into all kinds of interesting stuff with rental cars."

"Mostly just stains on the back seat covers. But we can take those out and wash them."

"Sounds delightful."

"Hey, dude, you got anything to smoke?"

"What, like a cigarette?"

"That would be good."

"I roll my own, but you're welcome to one."

"Cool!"

"We'll have to go around front to my truck."

"Let's motate, dude!"

Jimmy and I went around the office trailer to the parking area, and I rolled him a cigarette. He was mesmerized.

"No way, dude! How did you do that one-handed? It's like a magic trick!"

"I've been at it for several years. Practice makes perfect."

"You're cool, dude! Can you show me how to do that?"

"I don't have time right now, but if I get back this way again, I'll make sure I bring along some extra papers and tobacco. Then we'll see how you do."

"Bitchin'! If my chick sees me do that, she'll go orgasmic!"

"You better get back to work, Jimmy, before Carrot catches you goofing off."

"He's pretty slack, but you're probably right. Later, dude."

I fired up my truck and hit the road. I wanted to get back to Palmer Lake and talk to Travis, to fill him in on the details about the black Caddy.

When I got to the barbershop, Travis was playing checkers with Toot. By the look on Travis's face, Toot was winning.

"Travis, I need to talk to you. Can you guys take a break?"

"Sure. I've had it with these damn checkers, anyhow."

"Good, cause this has to do with Diamond Car Rentals."

"Toot, I've got important business to conduct with Corky. We'll have to call it done for today."

"Travis, you always cut me off when you're losing. Your business with Corky is probably about as important as duck droppings. Before I leave, I'm going to use the head. Something is screaming to get out."

"Like duck droppings?"

Toot headed for the restroom, but he didn't quite make it there before a noisy one slipped out.

"Well, Corky, was it worth the trip to Diamond, or was it a bust?"

"Travis, the Caddy is back on their lot! And I found out some stuff that definitely ties in with the Torrelli mystery!"

"So, speak!"

"I talked to Carrot. He's the guy who owns the place."

"Carrot? Was the guy eating one?"

"No, I guess he's had that nickname since he was a little kid."

"Who the hell would want to be called Carrot? That's like calling a girl named Kitty, Pussy!"

"Travis, do you know any girls named Kitty?"

"Let's not get off track, Corky. What did Carrot have to say?"

"He remembered Torrelli, alright. Apparently, Nicky made him feel a bit uncomfortable with his attitude and all."

"I can relate."

"Torrelli paid him up front in cash for a week's rental on the car. Then some other guy returned the Caddy a few days early, and told Carrot that Torrelli had to leave town unexpectedly. When Carrot tried to give him some money back, he hopped on the back of a waiting motorcycle and sped off!"

"A motorcycle? You mean there was someone else in on it, too?"

"That's what it sounds like."

"What else did he tell you?"

"He said the guy who brought the car back was short and pudgy, and was wearing a dirty bowling shirt. The lot boy, Jimmy, said the Caddy smelled like old gas inside, and they were having to let it air out."

"Corky, that makes me think of someone we know!"

"Who?"

"Mama's little boy, Leroy!"

"Oh, no!"

"What?"

"I just thought of something. Carrot said he couldn't see the motorcycle driver's face because of the helmet, but he noticed tattoo-covered arms."

"So?"

"Lorraine rides a motorcycle and has tattoo-covered arms. And she works for Leroy!"

"Corky, when you told me about her, I figured she was trouble. Girls like that have a lot of secrets."

"Hey, Travis, cool it. Here comes Toot."

Toot assured Travis that he would return to beat him at checkers once again, then bid us farewell. Unfortunately, the ghost from the restroom followed him out.

"Travis, how can you stand that? He stinks up the place something fierce!"

Travis started laughing, and then he pulled a pair of plugs out of his nose.

"Are you kidding me?"

"I'm just a nice guy, Corky."

"I guess!"

"So, did you learn anything else from your visit to Diamond?"

"You want to hear about the free popcorn?"

"Why don't you keep that part a secret."

"Hey, Travis, maybe you should have a popcorn

machine in here. That smell would sure be a lot better than Toot's!"

"Corky, next you'll have me showing movies!"

"Travis, that reminds me, did you give any more thought to visiting Charlene? Maybe you should take her to Keselburg for an X-rated movie! That would get things heated up for dinner!"

"I'm still trying to remember which one of the Troublemakers' albums she heard in my van. I've got five different ones."

"Why not take all five?"

"I want her to remember it just the way it was."

"I got the feeling that Charlene's diet hasn't included men for a while. I think any of the albums will do just fine."

"You think so, do you? Since when are you such an authority on women, Corky?"

"Travis, I'm heading out to the Palmers' to see if I can get paid. Do you want me to stop at Charlene's and give her a message?"

"No, thanks."

"I'm kind of afraid she's going to point her shotgun at me when I drive by, and pull the trigger, if she doesn't hear from you soon."

"Well, maybe you should rent the black Caddy, so she doesn't recognize you."

"That's a good idea!"

I left the barbershop and headed home so I could drop off the stuff from Jumbo's and write up a bill for the Palmers'.

While I was there, I figured I better feed my cat. When I was getting her food out of the cabinet, I spotted a couple of leftover cupcakes from D.J. Martin's housewarming party last year.

D.J. had to move out of the trailer park into a real house, after his next-door neighbor's barbeque exploded and burnt his place to the ground. I went by to see it after the fire was out, and all that was left was a dog dish sitting atop a pile of ashes.

I grabbed the cupcakes and took them with me on my drive out to the Palmers'. It's a good thing I carry a jug of water in my truck - those cupcakes were mighty crunchy! I think I chipped a tooth!

Chapter Eighteen

When I pulled into the circular driveway at the Palmer house, I noticed the addition of a new piece of artwork in the middle of the pond. It was a naked peeing boy statue. I'd heard about them before, but this was the first time I'd ever seen one.

The boy appeared to be about six years old, however, his unit was the size of a mature teenager's. That must be the necessary size required to handle the two gallons-per-minute flow rate.

I decided not to pass up the opportunity to top off my cooling system, and opened the hood of my truck, popped off the radiator cap and pulled forward. It only took a few seconds to fill it, and as I was backing up, I heard a familiar voice.

"Corky Perkins, you get your old truck away from my fountain right this minute!"

It was the one and only Anita. She had been on

the other side of the bushes planting flowers, so I hadn't seen her.

"Anita, I don't know what came over me."

"You're perverted!"

"It must be the medication I'm on."

"I think you need medication, Corky!"

"I got bit by a poisonous spider, and my doctor has me on some stuff that makes me drift off absentmindedly."

"And just where did this so-called poisonous spider bite you?"

"I was in a customer's attic."

"I don't mean that! Where on your body did you get bit?"

"In my privates."

"Oh!"

"I guess that's what attracted me to the fountain. I'm jealous of that boy being able to pee without it hurting. The doctor told me that some spider bites can even cause it to fall off."

"Sick!"

Anita was looking rather pale again. My bullshit story about the spider bite worked like a charm. No more bitching me out about my truck!

"Why are you here, Corky?"

"I came by to see about getting paid."

"I thought Aaron already paid you!"

"I haven't given him the bill yet. I brought it with me."

"Well, let's go get this taken care of."

Getting invited in was a real surprise, since I had a spider bite!

Anita had me wait in the entry while she went to get Aaron. I'd been in here once before, but I didn't remember seeing this one painting. It had several naked women sunning themselves around a pool. Just as I was deciding which one of the girls I would like to jump in the water with, Anita returned.

"Corky, Aaron will be with you in a minute. Why don't you have a seat?"

She left the room again, and I immediately went back to gazing at the skinny dippers. I was about to ask one of the girls to help me with my shorts, when Aaron came in.

"Corky, I'm Aaron Palmer. Anita tells me you've been doing some work on the barn, and she speaks very highly of you."

Anita speaks highly of me? The spider bite medicine must be affecting my hearing!

"I'm glad to finally meet you, Aaron. I've heard your name mentioned in conversation several times."

"Being the grandson of Palmer Lake's founder, I'm sure the conversations were anything but complimentary."

"I know the feeling. I installed a heavy-duty seat on a customer's toilet last month, because four-hundred-pound Aunt Bessie was coming to visit. Then they called back, and blamed me for the thing not flushing down a week's worth of her road trip snacks."

"I see."

"Just be glad you didn't see!"

"Corky, I understand you brought our bill."

"It's right here in the envelope."

"Did you get everything done that Anita wanted?"

"Well, I took care of everything on her list."

"Why don't you have a seat, and I'll go write you a check."

I was hoping I'd get more time alone with the painting, and now was my chance. I was getting to know one of the girls on a first-name basis.

When Aaron returned, he handed me a check for the full amount. I thanked him, and then started for the door.

"Corky, have you got a few minutes?"

"What's up?"

"I'd like you to show me what you did at the barn. Anita doesn't seem to want to take the time."

"Sure."

I was surprised Aaron wanted to spend time with me, being so high and mighty. He went to go change his shoes, and left me alone with the painted girls again. He was gone just long enough for me to be able to give one of them a pat on the bum.

During our trip down to the barn, Aaron didn't

speak a word. It reminded me of hearing about guys who can't walk and chew gum. When we got there, I gave him the twenty-five-cent tour, and he continued with his silent act, until I showed him the window.

"Anita had you put in a window?"

"She told me she wanted to be able to see some kid shoveling horse manure."

"You've got to be kidding!"

"Aaron, it was just another thing on her list."

"Why would she need a window for that?"

"You'll have to take that up with her. I learned pretty quick not to voice my opinion."

"So, is that everything you did here?"

"Well, not quite. I saved the best for last. Welcome to Anita's pride and joy."

"What in the world is that?"

"This is her all-electric toilet."

"Corky, did you talk her into this?"

"Aaron, I'd never even heard of an electric toilet before. Anita told me her friend has one in their barn, and that's how she got the idea."

"An electric toilet?"

"It's really an incinerator. It burns everything up and turns it to ash. Anita wanted it because the ashes are good for the garden."

"That woman is out of her mind!"

"No comment."

"Corky, when we first moved in, I used to keep a riding lawnmower in here. I really enjoyed driving it, and it only took about fifteen minutes to mow the grass. But, when I was gone out of town for a week, Anita had a landscaper triple the size of our lawn. Now we have someone else take care of it."

I could see that Aaron was reliving an unhappy memory, so I left him alone for a minute.

We finished our show-and-tell session at the barn and headed back toward the house. Aaron had gone quiet again, so I decided to see if I could break the silence.

"Aaron, do you ride the horses?"

"No. I tried it once, but that was a disaster."

"What happened?"

"Anita took me on the trail through the woods, and I got bit by mosquitoes and scratched by sticker bushes. Plus, my ass was sore for three days!"

"I know about the sore ass thing. That happened to me one time when I went roller skating."

"How do you get a sore ass from roller skating?"

"I lost control and went down a flight of concrete stairs on my rear end."

"Ouch!"

"Then my girlfriend dumped me because I couldn't perform in bed! It was too painful."

"So, you understand how women behave, too."

"I thought I did, until I met Anita."

"What makes her any different?"

"While I was working on the barn the other

day, I heard her screaming and yelling at some guy on the deck. I watched her chase him around the side of your house, then heard tires squealing and saw a black car leave your driveway."

We reached the house, and Aaron wanted me to come in. He asked me to take a seat, and then he called out for Anita.

"Aaron, what is it now? I'm right in the middle of reading my vending machine magazine."

"Anita, Corky said you had a visitor."

"Why is he still here? Didn't you pay him?"

"Yes, I paid him."

"A visitor? I have visitors all the time!"

"I know about your riding instructor, and a couple girls you go riding with, but they're not who I'm referring to."

"I don't have time for these games, Aaron! I'm sure you and Mr. Handyman think this is real funny!"

I felt like I was being squeezed in a bench vise. I didn't know Aaron would confront Anita and stick me in the middle. So, I stood up and walked over to the door.

"Corky, don't leave."

"Aaron, I've got a job to get to. The visitor was Nicky Torrelli."

I went outside and hopped in my truck. I had the key in the ignition and was about to start up the old beast when Aaron came running out of the house.

"Tell me everything you know about Torrelli!"

He stuck his hand through my open window and tucked a hundred-dollar bill in my shirt pocket!

"There's more where that came from."

I opened my door and got out of the truck.

"Aaron, Torrelli showed up again during your Canada trip."

I told him about the foul odor, and Leroy sending me on a wild goose chase, and then ended by telling him about Torrelli's dead body in the blackberries.

"Corky, you really expect me to believe that?"

"I don't care if you believe me or not! I came out here to work on a barn, not to get mixed up with some dead guy!"

"You're serious!"

"Aaron, you can think whatever you want. I'm out of here!"

"Wait a minute, Corky. I want you to show me where his body is."

"Aaron, his body isn't there anymore."

"Well, that's convenient. Corky, if he really was here, then I've got big trouble."

"How much trouble can a dead guy be?"

Aaron threw up his arms and shook his fists at the sky. Then he begged me to show him where I had found the body, even though it wasn't there anymore. So, we headed off towards the barn again.

As we walked down the gravel lane, I noticed a new planter in the Lacomes' yard. True to Lacome style, it was a huge, rusty old cast iron bathtub with flowers planted in it. I guess Leroy and Mama have good taste after all, since it matched the color of the broken-down vehicles around their place.

When we got down by the barn, I continued to lead the way into the woods. We arrived at the blackberries where Torrelli's body once was, but now, only the rolled up mattress was there.

"Corky, what's that doing here?"

"I don't know. This is where his body was."

"He's not inside that thing, is he?"

"You want to take a look?"

"Corky, if Torrelli is really dead, I want to see proof."

"Well, I've got my pocket knife."

I cut the ropes loose from the mattress, and it slowly unrolled like a fat chick I once knew. The mattress was filthy on the outside from being dragged through the dirt, and the inside was all stained with what looked like motor oil. But there was no body inside.

"Corky, if you really did find Torrelli's body here, what did you do?"

"I wanted to call the sheriff, but you guys were gone to Canada, and there was nobody home at the Lacomes', so I couldn't use the phone. I drove all the way back to town and found my friend Travis, and he came back out here with me and confirmed that the guy was really dead."

"How did you know it was Torrelli?"

"Travis recognized his haircut. The guy had been in his barbershop a few days earlier."

"Did you tell the sheriff?"

"No. I didn't want to spend the time trying to find him. But we spotted him the next morning pulling into the Bite Time, and got him to come out here and take a look. Unfortunately, by that time, the body was gone, and all that was here was this mattress."

"Corky, I'm sure you realize how hard it is for me to believe this."

"Well, the sheriff didn't believe a word of it, either, since there wasn't a body."

Aaron and I left the woods and headed back to the house. During our walk, he told me not to speak about it to anyone. I'm sure he didn't believe a word I said.

I headed back for town, figuring the Palmers would probably never hire me again. I was going to miss seeing Anita, sort of the same way I miss the burning bag of dog crap someone put on my front porch last Halloween. But at least I got paid. And, I even got an extra hundred!

Chapter Nineteen

As I drove away from the Palmers', I felt like going to Bertha's and getting drunk. I was well aware that Travis and I were destined to be the laughing stock of Palmer Lake, thanks to Sheriff Drew, and really pissed that I was even involved in this whole mess. Why did I have to be the one to find the body, anyhow?

A mile down the road, a police car appeared in my rearview mirror. I didn't think much of it, until the lights and siren came on. I pulled my old beast to a screeching halt on the shoulder, and damn near slid into the ditch. Then up to my window came none other than Sheriff Drew. What was he doing way out here?

"Okay, Perkins, out of the truck!"

"What for, Sheriff? I wasn't speeding."

"Out of the truck, now!"

"You been watching reruns of Highway Patrol again, Sheriff?"

Next thing I knew, he'd opened my door, pulled me out of the truck, and slammed me up against the fender.

"Listen, handy-boy, I got word that you've been bothering the Palmers. You stay away from them, and quit asking questions around town about them. Do you understand me?"

He pushed me down on the ground before going back to his patrol car and leaving.

I stayed in the dirt until Drew was out of sight, then got back on my feet, brushed off the dust, and walked around the other side of my truck and took a leak. Ever since the spider bite, being scared has affected my bladder.

I got back in my truck, and now there was no doubt in my mind that I would be heading to Bertha's.

I pulled in the parking lot, feeling kind of beat up. All I wanted to do was have a drink and bitch to somebody before I went nuts. I spotted Billy Hamrod outside having a smoke, and figured he'd be the guy. But, as I headed his direction, here came Pinkie and Rosie. They started kissing him and putting their hands in his pockets. So, I went inside, grabbed a seat at the bar, and ordered a beer.

I really needed someone to talk to, and I kept looking for a familiar face. As I scanned the place for the third time, I noticed outside that the Buettemeier girls had their backs against the front window with their shirts pulled up! Billy Boy was planting kiss after kiss!

I slammed my beer down on the bar and let out five of my best French words. Then someone tapped me on the back.

"Corky, I haven't heard language like that since I got caught playing doctor with the neighbor girl!"

"Travis! Do you see what's going on out front?"

"Well, I'll be dipped. He's sure got the touch, doesn't he?"

"I should be the one out there with those girls, not that antique!"

"Corky, don't tell me that's why you're so upset?"

"That's not the real reason, but it doesn't help."

"Trust me, once they've bled old Billy dry, they'll move on to someone new."

Travis signaled to Bertha for a round and took a seat at the bar. He's never come clean about his connection with the Buettemeier sisters, and I suspect that he was in their custody at some point.

"So, Corky, are you going to keep what's bugging you a secret the rest of your life?"

"I got pulled over by Sheriff Drew on the way here. He roughed me up and told me that I better keep my nose out of other people's business!"

"Like who?"

"The Palmers!"

"Why, that lazy sack of shit! He pushed you around?"

"Right there on the side of the road!"

Turning all red and sweaty, Travis started cussing about Drew, calling him names I'd never heard before. Then he began pointing at the front window, calling the Buettemeier sisters the same names!

Now we were drawing attention from the whole place. Bertha was polite at first about it, but Travis ignored her, so she ramped it up a notch and insisted we behave. It took a couple more drinks each to finally calm down, and by that time, Billy and the Buettemeiers had moved on.

"Travis, I don't think anyone's buying our dead guy story. Aaron Palmer wanted me to show him where I found the body, but when he saw the mattress, I'm sure he thought I was blowing smoke up his ass."

"What about Anita?"

"I wouldn't mind blowing smoke up her ass. She was being her usual, bitchy self, because I filled my radiator in her peeing boy fountain!"

"You pissed in her fountain?"

"That's not what I said, Travis."

"Sounded like it to me."

Travis changed the subject and started to tell me about his conversations with Attorney Claymore and Mary Ellen Smythe. He had barely got rolling,

TROUBLE COMES TO PALMER LAKE

when in walked Leroy and Mama, followed by Lorraine and another gal. At the site of Lorraine, my whole attitude changed.

"Hey, Travis, check out the long hair and tattoos! That's Lorraine!"

"Corky, get a load of that greasy old jacket that Leroy has on. Can you imagine wanting to wear a dirty thing like that?"

"Screw Leroy. Lorraine's the most beautiful creature I've ever seen!"

"Didn't you just tell me that you wanted to be the one outside licking the Buttmore sisters?"

"Come on, Travis. Let's go over and pull up a chair at their table. You really need to see her tattoos!"

"Corky, you might have the hots for her, but I'm not interested in Lorraine, or her tattoos. I want to talk to Leroy. And Corky, your tongue belongs inside your mouth, not hanging out like a stray dog."

We wandered over to their table, and Travis put on his gentleman's charm.

"Good evening, Mrs. Lacome. Lovely dress you're wearing."

"Why, thank you, Travis. Nice of you to notice. Two dollars on the thrift store clearance rack in Keselburg."

"Mind if we pull up a couple of chairs and have a drink with you folks?"

"Sounds like a good idea. Travis, have you met Lorraine and Debra?"

"I have not had the pleasure."

"Lorraine, Debra, this is Travis O'Riley, the town barber."

"Evening, girls. I'd like you to meet my friend Corky Perkins. He's our local handyman. If your plumbing's plugged up, he's your guy!"

"Thanks, Travis."

"So, Leroy, where did you find that fancy jacket?"

"This old thing? I've had it for twenty years, Travis. It's my favorite one for working on cars."

"I couldn't help but notice all the grease and oil stains. Kind of reminds me of a mattress I once saw."

"An old mattress is good to have around if you're going to be working under cars and trucks. I keep a couple of them in my garage at home."

"You wouldn't happen to be missing one of them, would you?"

"Missing a mattress? What are you talking about?"

"Corky, do you want to tell Leroy, or should I? Corky!"

I was as far away from Travis's conversation as the planet Mars is from Palmer Lake. My eyes were glued to Lorraine.

"What? Did you say something to me, Travis?"

"Never mind."

"What?"

"Leroy, Corky and I came across an old mattress in the woods behind the Palmers' barn. You remember the Palmers, don't you? They live right next door to you."

"I don't know nothing about what goes on over there."

"Well, Leroy, I'm sure Aaron Palmer doesn't keep oil-stained mattresses around his place. Kind of clashes with the putting green."

"Mama, I think it's time we head home."

"But we just got here, son."

Leroy started to get up, and Travis grabbed him and pushed him back in his chair.

"You're not going anywhere, grease ball!"

"Travis O'Riley, you leave my boy alone!"

"Mrs. Lacome, Leroy has something he needs to get off his chest."

"Travis, Mama told you to leave me alone!"

Then Lorraine stood up. I figured she and Debra weren't going to hang around if there was going to be an altercation between Leroy and Travis. But, to my surprise, she started in lecturing Leroy!

"Leroy, you better come clean if you don't want to wind up taking the heat for something you didn't do. Take it from Debra and me - we both landed in women's prison, because we tried to protect other people. The only good thing to come of it was that we met and fell in love."

Then Lorraine planted a little kiss on Debra's

cheek. I thought I was going to puke! I had no idea that Lorraine and Debra were joined below the belt! Now I understood what Mama Lacome meant about real women!

"Travis, I'm gonna go take a piss!"

Chapter Twenty

Travis told me later that he thought he should teach me some manners. As far as he was concerned, I didn't need to tell everyone in the place that I needed to take a piss! But he was too busy interrogating Leroy to do anything about it.

In his younger days, Travis wanted to grow up and be a police detective. His girlfriend at the time, Ruth Ann, had an uncle who was a motorcycle cop. One evening when Travis was walking home from her place, Officer Russell Helens had a car stopped, and was in an argument with the driver.

Travis snuck behind some bushes to get closer to the action, and he spotted the police motorcycle. It was still running, and the lights were flashing. That was all it took. He ran out, hopped on Uncle Russ's motorcycle, and off he sped. He got caught a few miles later, and that ended any chance of him ever becoming a cop.

Tonight at Bertha's, though, Travis was getting to play detective by giving Leroy the third degree. That mama's boy was guilty of something having to do with Nicky Torrelli, and Travis was going to squeeze it out of him.

"Alright, Leroy, you've had enough cuddling. You know all about that dirty mattress we found at the Palmers'. Now, confess!"

"I didn't do it!"

"Yes, you did, Leroy!"

"I didn't kill nobody!"

"So you do know about the dead guy!"

"I just did what I was told to, Travis. I moved the body, because Cousin Jimmy said if I didn't get it off their property, Miss Anita would get in trouble!"

"Who the hell is Cousin Jimmy?"

"He's my cousin!"

"Does Cousin Jimmy have a last name?"

"Yeah."

"Well, what is it, Leroy?"

"Wiseman."

"Wiseman? He wouldn't be the same Jimmy Wiseman who works at Diamond Car Rentals, would he?"

"Travis, how do you know where my cousin works?"

Travis had old Leroy spilling his guts! Now he was thinking he should have changed his name and become a cop, after all!

"Okay, Leroy, I want the story behind the rolled-up mattress."

"Mama, he knows where Cousin Jimmy works!"

Leroy moved closer to Mama, and started shaking like a battery-operated vibrator.

"Tell me about the mattress, Leroy!"

"It was in the back of my station wagon, and the dead guy's body wouldn't fit in there with it. So, I rolled it up and put it in the woods."

"You used your car to move the dead guy?"

"I had to. He was too heavy to carry. It was all I could do just to drag him out of the woods!"

"What did you do with him after you got him in your car?"

"Nothing."

"Leroy, you lie!"

"I just drove him back to my garage!"

"Is that what Jimmy told you to do?"

"He told me to leave the guy in the car, and he would take care of it."

"Did Jimmy show up?"

"I guess so."

"You guess so?"

"Well, dead guys can't get out of cars on their own, can they?"

Travis had gotten Leroy talking, but then Leroy decided to get cocky, like he was some kind of a celebrity.

"Mrs. Lacome, would you please instruct your

son to answer my questions without being a smart-ass?"

"Travis, Leroy has had enough of your questions. You remind me of a cop."

"I'll take that as a compliment, Mrs. Lacome."

"You can take it any way you want to. As for us, we're taking it out of here. Come on, Leroy, Lorraine, Debra, we're leaving!"

The four of them got up and split. That really pissed Travis off. He signaled Bertha to bring him another shot.

Chapter Twenty-One

While Travis was trying to squeeze Leroy for information, the news from Lorraine came out. I thought it might be a diversion on her part to get Travis off Leroy's ass. But then she put her arm around Debra, and gave her a little kiss on the cheek. How could such a good-looking gal, with such great tattoos, have the cream jeans for another chick?

In the men's room, I stood at the urinal pretending the deodorizer block was Lorraine.

"Take that, you faker!"

As I was hosing her down, a guy who looked like he'd been drinking all day came out of the stall. I'd been wondering what was causing the rotten smell, and the mirror to fog.

"Who you talking to, cowboy?"

We struck up a conversation and I told him about Lorraine's coming out party. Then the guy stumbled over to the urinal and started spitting on the deodorant block.

"Take that, you phony broad!"

As I was reaching for the can of air freshener by the sink, in walked another guy. The place was getting crowded with three of us in there. Before I knew it, the first guy started telling this newcomer about Lorraine. Then he pointed to the urinal and told him to let her have it. The newcomer did as instructed, giving the deodorant block a good rinse down while voicing his opinions. The three of us wound up shaking hands, and walked out feeling extremely manly.

After what I'd seen and heard from Lorraine, I had no desire to hang around Bertha's any longer. As I was headed for the door, I spotted Travis, sitting all by himself at the table.

"Where the hell have you been, Corky? You missed all of it! Leroy confessed!"

"Leroy confessed? I think you've got it all wrong, Travis. Lorraine is the one who confessed!"

"Well, that's true. But old Leroy spilled the beans! He's the one who moved Torrelli's body from the woods, and put the mattress there!"

"He told you that?"

"Only after I put the screws to him."

"Travis, would you not use the word 'screw.' It makes me think about Lorraine and Debra."

"Sorry, Corky."

"So, where are they, anyway?"

"I pissed off Mama Lacome, giving Leroy the third degree. So she gave the order to leave. Corky, I knew I should have become a cop!"

"So, what happened to the body?"

"Leroy used his car to move it from the woods to his garage. Then his cousin took over. I know you're not going to believe this, but his cousin is Jimmy Wiseman!"

"From Carrot's place?"

"One and the same!"

Travis went on and on, telling me the details of Leroy's confession over another round of drinks. Then we decided it would be a good idea for me to pay another visit to Diamond Car Rentals as soon as possible.

Chapter Twenty-Two

The next morning, I was getting ready to head to Keselburg to track down Jimmy Wiseman. Since Travis learned about his connection to Leroy, I was anxious to see if I could get Jimmy to spill the beans. I figured rolling him a couple cigarettes would do the trick.

Syrup was dripping off my chin, as I hurried to finish my breakfast waffle. I was about halfway done when my phone started ringing.

"This is Corky."

"Is this Corky, the handyman?"

"You're talking to him."

"Corky, my name is Lee Rogerson. I got your name and number from Robin Marie, at the clinic in Keselburg. She says you're the guy to call to fix a toilet."

"The VD clinic?"

"That's right. Why? Does that make a difference?"

TROUBLE COMES TO PALMER LAKE

"Just making sure."

"Corky, I own the radio station here in town, and we only have a single bathroom in this place. Last night, I had a get-together with one of our sponsors, and now the toilet is plugged up. Can you be of help? It's a real emergency."

"You aren't Lee Rogerson the disc jockey, are you?"

"You listen to KRUD?"

"In my truck, I do."

"Yes, I'm him."

"Well, it's your lucky day! I'm heading to Keselburg this morning to take care of some business. Where are you located?"

"Do you know where Holly's Nail Salon is?"

"Holly's? No, I don't think I do."

"How about the Chicken Shack restaurant?"

"I've been by there before."

"We're right across the street from the Shack, behind Holly's, in a small brick building. Actually, it's a converted garage in the alley. Our KRUD sign is on the door."

"How long can you hold it, Lee?"

"That's the problem. I put a lot of whipped cream and caramel syrup on my oatmeal this morning."

"Well, how about you play a whole side of an album while you run across the street to the Chicken Shack and use their facilities."

"That's a great idea! I was figuring on going to

Holly's, but she doesn't open till noon. I'll probably make some of our listeners mad, playing a whole side of an album. But what's a guy to do?"

"It is a country station, Lee. No one will even notice."

"What the hell does that mean?"

"Have a cup of coffee, and I'll see you in an hour."

I finished my cold waffle, then loaded the plumbing tools in my truck and headed for Keselburg. During the drive, I couldn't stop thinking about Lorraine. How disappointing to find out that she and Debra were a couple. I thought those kinds of girls only lived in big cities, not in small towns where nothing ever happens!

The Chicken Shack was on the corner of the first intersection I came to in Keselburg. I looked across the street, and sure enough, there was Holly's place. I parked my truck in front of the restaurant, grabbed my tools, and walked down the alley.

The KRUD place was pretty small, and when I walked in, the familiar smell hit me immediately. There was a guy sitting in a beat-up lawn chair behind a folding table that had a record player and a microphone on it. He was in the middle of doing a commercial for a gun shop, and when he finished, he started a record.

"Hello there. Can I help you?"

"Well, actually, I'm here to help you."

"Corky?"

"Yes, sir."

"Thank god! The bathroom is through that door."

"Lee, I could find it with my eyes closed. It must be hard to sit here and have to breathe that."

"Tell me about it. I've been here since four this morning. Corky, how long before it's fixed?"

"Hopefully before you pass out."

"I think some of the records are starting to warp."

"You know something, Lee? You don't look anything like you sound on the radio."

"So I've been told."

"Other than that baseball cap, you kind of remind me of Kriss Kringle."

"We're related."

"Well, I'll get started with the repair."

"Corky, try not to make a lot of noise. We're on the air. And no swearing."

"You must know my reputation!"

It wound up taking me a couple hours to fix the problem, because I had to take the toilet off the floor to unplug it. To my surprise, I found a pair of women's panties stuck in the trap!

Just for fun, I rinsed the panties out in the sink, and put them in a clear plastic bag I found on one of the bathroom shelves. As I was leaving, I dropped them on the table next to the microphone. Lee got a big grin on his face, but kept right on announcing.

As I was carrying my tools back to the truck, the thought came to me that maybe I should offer Jimmy Wiseman lunch at the Chicken Shack. If I bought him a meal, he might be more talkative.

Diamond Car Rentals was only about a half-mile from the radio station, so it didn't take long to get there. As I walked in the door, I immediately smelled the popcorn, even though my nose was still dripping from the toilet job.

Carrot was behind the counter picking at something on his sport coat, and he didn't notice me come in.

"Howdy, Carrot."

"Oh, sorry. Hey, I remember you. You're the investigator!"

"You have a good memory."

"Popcorn's on. Want some?"

"No, thanks. I was wondering if I might speak with your lot boy again?"

"Jimmy? Sure, he's out back."

When I rounded the corner of the office, I spotted Jimmy, bent over cleaning the back seat of one of the rental cars. His butt crack was in full view, and for some reason, it made me think of Lorraine and Debra.

"Jimmy, is that you in there?"

"Hey, dude!"

"Find anything interesting in the back seat today?"

"Just a couple of candy bar wrappers. Hey, I forgot your name."

"Does Corky ring your chimes?"

"Corky! Ding dong, dude!"

"Jimmy, have you ever eaten at the Chicken Shack?"

"Oh, dude, that is the best place on the planet! My mouth even waters when I hear their commercials on the radio!"

"How about I take you to lunch there?"

"Don't mess with my head, dude!"

"I'm not messing with you, Jimmy. I'd like to buy you lunch in exchange for some information about the rental car business. Can you get away for an hour?"

"Just watch me!"

We went around to the front of the office, and Jimmy stuck his head in the door to tell Carrot he was taking his lunch break. Carrot was still picking at his jacket, but he stopped just long enough to give Jimmy the thumbs-up signal.

"Hey, dude, your truck smells kind of funky."

"How about you drop the dude, and just call me Corky. The truck smells like my last job."

"Can I bum a smoke? Maybe it'll clear away the stink."

"You know, I only carry the roll-your-own type."

"Pot? Cool, man!"

"No, Jimmy, not pot. Here, I brought along an

extra package of tobacco so you can practice."

I handed him the papers and the tobacco, and he looked perplexed.

"What should I do?"

"Give it back. I'll roll you one."

I started rolling cigarettes at the age of fourteen, because my girlfriend at the time was a pro at it. She showed me the basics, but the rest was years of practice on my part. Jimmy wanted to know if she was fourteen, too.

"She was older than I was, but she'd never tell me her age. She always avoided the question."

Jimmy sat up straight and lit the cigarette.

"Dude, I've got a thing going with an older woman, too. She doesn't roll her own smokes, but she's fun to roll in the sack with!"

"I can relate. How old are you, Jimmy?"

"Nineteen, last month."

I assumed the girl must have been a teenager when they got together, probably a year or two ahead of him in school. And with Jimmy being on the heavy side, his girlfriend was probably chubby and desperate.

When we arrived at the Chicken Shack, we had our pick of places to sit. The lunch menu included every kind of chicken dish one could want, as long as you liked barbeque. Jimmy's eyes grew to twice their normal size as he read the selections.

"Dude, you should try the number eleven."

"Sounds like you're a regular here."

"Carrot pays me every Friday, and after work, this is where I come."

"So, tell me, Jimmy, are you and the older gal still together?"

"Oh, yeah."

"Since you're still too young to get into the bars and taverns, you two must go to the movies a lot."

"No, we just get together at her house and fool around. Sometimes we'll watch one of her videos, but usually after messing around, she falls asleep."

"So, what do you do when she's asleep?"

"I grab something from the refrigerator, then I split."

"That's it?"

"Pretty much."

When we finished our lunch, we both needed to wash our hands. The barbeque sauce was pretty messy. While we were in the men's room cleaning up, I noticed a condom dispenser on the wall.

"Hey, Jimmy, I'll bet the real reason you come here when you get paid is so you can stock up on rubbers. You and your older girlfriend must go through a lot of those."

"No way! I come here for the chicken, dude! Anyhow, she can't get pregnant."

That made me curious, but I figured I shouldn't pry. I'd heard stories about chubby chicks not being able to conceive because the fat pinched off their pipes.

When we climbed in my truck, Jimmy asked if I would roll him another one-handed smoke.

"Hey, dude, how long did it really take to learn how to do that?"

"It took quite a few packages of tobacco before I quit making a big mess. It was pretty frustrating, especially since Mary Beth could do it so perfectly."

Jimmy started laughing. When he finally calmed down, I asked him what was so funny?

"Hey, dude, you were hanging out with an older girl named Mary?"

"Yeah. Why is that so funny?"

"Cause, the gal I'm hanging out with is named Mary!"

"Really?"

"Girls named Mary must have a thing for younger guys, dude!"

"Jimmy, my girlfriend got pissed if I called her Mary. She insisted that I call her Mary Beth."

Jimmy started laughing again.

"That's crazy, man! My chick gets pissed off at me for the same reason! Her name is Mary Ellen, but if I call her Mary, she really gets bent!"

"No kidding? Maybe they're related?"

"Honest, dude. How flipping weird is that, anyhow?"

"Hey, have you ever messed around with her in your car?"

"No. My car is too full of junk. We did try it in

her car once, right after she first got it."

"Jimmy, do you have any relatives around these parts?"

"Yeah, but I don't get along with most of them."

"Do your parents live around here?"

"Yeah, they live in Keselburg."

"Do you get along with them?"

"Not really. My dad's still mad at me because I didn't want to be an electrician like he is."

"Where's he work?"

"At Keselburg Electric."

"I find electrical work kind of fascinating. Did you ever give it a try?"

"I went on some side jobs with him for a while, but when I'd screw up, he'd get really ticked off."

"Did you learn anything, or was it a total waste of time?"

"I figured out some stuff, but he wanted me to go to trade school and learn everything. He talked about us starting a business together, but I just couldn't handle the thought of working with my old man the rest of my life."

"Relatives can be a real pain in the ass sometimes. They always want to tell you how to live. Do you have any plans for the future?"

"I've always wanted to drive long-haul trucks. I figured it would take me a couple years to save up for school, but now, I don't have to. Mary Ellen just gave me the money."

"Really?"

I wanted to name-drop Cousin Leroy, but I figured it might scare him off. So I started in about the rental car business instead.

"Jimmy, I was wondering what happens to a rental car after it gets a lot of miles on it. Does Diamond just keep on renting them until they die?"

"No, man. They go to the auction when they get about fifty thousand miles on them. But the classic old ones, like the Caddy, rent for a lot more, so we keep them fixed up."

"That's pretty interesting. I didn't know they went to auction."

"The auctions are a gas to go to. You see all kinds of cars and people there. Mary Ellen bought her car there last year, and got a great deal! I taught her how to bid on them."

"You must be pretty smart."

"I've learned quite a bit about cars, working at Diamond."

"You have any good advice?"

"Don't try doing it in the back seat with your chick, dude! Mary Ellen got her hair caught in the door handle, and it wrecked our whole night!"

When we pulled into the Diamond lot, Jimmy thanked me for the lunch and the smokes, and then he headed around back. I stuck my head in the front door to thank Carrot for lending me his lot boy, but he was still picking at his jacket, so I decided not to disturb him.

TROUBLE COMES TO PALMER LAKE

I got back in my truck, tuned in KRUD on the radio, and then headed for home. A couple miles down the road, Lee dedicated a song to Corky the thong man! How cool, dude!

When I finally reached Palmer Lake, I headed straight for the barbershop. I pulled in the parking lot and could see the lights on and the door open, so I knew Travis was there. I walked in, and found him brushing his teeth at the sink.

"Getting ready for a hot date?"

"I'm trying to get a foul taste out of my mouth."

"What was her name?"

"Smart-ass. Toot stopped by after he'd had the taco special for lunch."

"It does kind of smell like Anita's manure pile in here."

"Oh, great! That should help my business!"

"Hey, Travis, I just came from Diamond Car Rentals."

"Oh yeah? Anything interesting to report?"

"Well, I took Jimmy out to lunch, but I didn't want to let on that I knew about him and Leroy, cause I figured he'd flip me off."

"So, what did you talk about?"

"Mostly women and cars."

"Maybe that's the best way to do it. Get him to think you guys are buddies, and then put him in the squeeze. Just like I did to Leroy."

"There is one thing he told me about that you might find interesting."

"That he's been banging his Aunt Mama?"

"Gross me out, Travis!"

"Just paying you back for the manure comment."

"Gee, thanks!"

"So, what did he have to say?"

"He told me he's been seeing an older woman for the last few years by the name of Mary Ellen."

"Mary Ellen? Mary Ellen who?"

"He didn't tell me her last name."

"Corky, how many gals do we know around these parts named Mary Ellen?"

"None, I don't think?"

"You're right about that - you don't think! What about Mary Ellen Smythe?"

"You don't really think it's that Mary Ellen, do you? She's way older than Jimmy. And she's not chubby."

"Did he mention any details of their relationship?"

"Oh, just the usual boy-girl stuff. He did tell me that he helped her get a car at the auction last year."

"What kind of a car?"

"He didn't say what brand, just that he helped her with the bidding."

This little bit of information seemed to stir Travis up. His face was getting kind of red, and that only happens when he gets excited.

"Corky, are you hungry?"

"Not at all. Why?"

"How about we go across the street to the Bite Time and have an early dinner."

"You must be dying for a taco."

"Smart-ass."

"Travis, I'll pass on the dinner offer. I'm still spitting feathers from my visit to the Chicken Shack."

"Corky, I think it would be a good idea if we planned a little trip for tonight. We've got some investigating to do."

"I'm not going back out to the Palmers'! One ass-whooping by the sheriff was one too many!"

"Calm down. We're not going there. We need to start looking in a whole new direction. How about we meet up at Bertha's around eight o'clock."

"You're going to keep me guessing till then?"

"Just meet me there at eight. And don't be late."

Travis closed up the shop and walked across the street to go eat. I got in my truck and headed for home, wondering what he had in mind for tonight.

Chapter Twenty-Three

Ever since I moved to Palmer Lake, I've heard lots of stories about our residents. When you live in a small town, people invent stuff about each other for recreation. Travis seems to be a regular target.

One story had to do with him being a guitar junkie. Supposedly, he had such a large collection that there wasn't enough room left in his house for a bed. So, he slept in his van.

Then there was the one about him being a collector of whiskey bottles. Again, he didn't have any room to sleep inside his house, because the whiskey bottles were stacked to the ceiling. In this version, he slept in a hammock in the neighbor's back yard, sometimes with the neighbor's wife.

But the tale that really got me was the one about him driving an ambulance in Keselburg. Travis would pick the pockets of the sick and injured men he transported, and then get friendly with their wives during their hospital stay. He was eventually run out of town, and that's how he wound up in Palmer Lake. With that kind of malarkey always floating around, it's hard to know what to believe.

After I got home from the barbershop, my first task was to clean the cat's litter box. Something must have crawled into it and died. The little strainer shovel got so clogged up that I had to finally throw it out. Thank goodness for rubber gloves.

There was a message on my answering machine about another toilet problem. That made twice in one day. This time it was from my sister, Belinda Suzie. Why she would be calling me is anybody's guess, since she lives over a hundred miles from Palmer Lake. But, from what I've gathered, her boyfriend isn't very handy. She met him at a county fair ten years ago when he was doing a magic act and telling fortunes. The fortune telling has long since disappeared, as well as the magic. He's now employed part-time as a bingo caller.

I phoned her back, letting it ring a dozen times before giving up. The two of them must be out on a date, probably at the next-door neighbor boy's tree fort, drinking.

After finishing up a couple loads of laundry, it was time to get ready to go meet Travis. As I was putting away my socks, I spotted my little thrift store camera in the drawer. If we were going out investigating, maybe it would be smart to get some pictures. I really scored, buying that camera. It was only two bucks. Then I found out that getting film for it was the reason it was so cheap.

Last month I spotted an estate sale sign, and picked up two five-packs of film for a buck. The old gal who had lived there died while shooting pool at the trailer park tournament, and her daughter was selling everything off. The film was a couple years past the expiration date, but the daughter said it should still be good since Mom had kept it in the freezer.

There certainly was no shortage of treasures around her place. Along with the film, I found a nice old handsaw, and a lawnmower spark plug still in the package. Travis stopped by and bought her entire record collection. He suffers from a vinyl addiction, and couldn't help himself.

It was getting close to eight o'clock, so I grabbed the camera and headed for Bertha's. I was hoping the Buettemeier sisters would be on display in the front window again so I could get a few shots before we went investigating.

Travis beat me there and was already on his second drink. I took the stool next to his and ordered up a beer, while keeping an eye out for the sisters.

After we finished our drinks, we headed to the parking lot.

"Corky, you want to ride on the back of my motorcycle, or should we take your truck?"

"Let's take the truck. Last time I rode on the back of your bike, you made me wear that stupid jacket."

"You mean the one that said, 'I like riding bitch?'"

"That's the one."

"Okay, then you drive."

"Travis, you haven't told me what we're up to yet."

"Well, after you left the barbershop, I made a few calls to some of my customers. My suspicions were right. I found out that Mary Ellen Smythe got her car at an auction. So, now, we're going to go do a little spying on her."

"You mean at her house?"

"Yeah. One of my regulars told me she lives on the far side of the lake. I figure, with any luck, we should be able to find it."

"It's getting kind of dark to be snooping around."

"I know that, but I do some of my best work in the dark. Just ask the Buttmore sisters."

"I knew it! Travis, you act like they don't mean anything to you every time I ask!"

"They don't mean anything to me, anymore. We had our fun for a few months, but then they found fresh meat and moved on."

"It wasn't Billy Hamrod, was it?"

"No, he came later. I didn't see them around for a while, so I got the feeling that it was probably some guy in Keselburg."

"Did they break your heart?"

"Corky, it wasn't my heart. Those two are like wild animals. When they were through with me, I needed the time off to heal up."

"So, why didn't you ever tell me about hanging out with them? I must have asked you a million times!"

"I've been done with them for over a year, and I didn't want to relive it by telling you stories."

"How bad could being with two loose women be?"

"Corky, those two are into every kind of toy, tool, and device known to man, along with snorting."

"They snort, too? They really must be wild animals!"

"They snort spray paint, hair spray, oven cleaner, and anything else that comes in a spray can! Now, can we just drive?"

"Was it fun?"

"It was, until the night one of them tried to bite off my little toe."

It took us about twenty minutes to get to the far side of the lake, and then we started looking for a road to turn on.

"Corky, there by that old boat trailer."

"That looks like a dirt trail, Travis."

"Yeah, but that's got to be it."

"Okay. But hold on. This is going to be a bumpy ride."

Bumpy wasn't the word for it. This little dirt

TROUBLE COMES TO PALMER LAKE

lane was full of potholes. We had to go really slow to keep from knocking our heads on the roof of my truck.

After a minute or two, we thought we spotted a house. When we got close enough, it actually turned out to be an old cabin that was about ready to fall down.

"Travis, you don't think she lives in that thing, do you?"

"I think the only thing living there probably died years ago. Let's keep going and see what else we can find."

We continued on, bouncing like a fat girl on a trampoline.

"Travis, look up ahead. I think I see a light."

"Where?"

"Over there, to your right."

"Park the truck. You got a flashlight?"

"Yeah, but it's got dead batteries."

"Well, I guess we'll have to be as careful as girl scouts then."

We quietly climbed out of the truck and started walking. Sure enough, we came to a driveway with a glowing lamppost and two cars.

"Hey, Corky, I think this is Mary Ellen's car. I recognize the stuffed raccoon in the back window."

"Take a look at this other car, Travis. The thing is crammed full of junk, and covered with bumper stickers. Look, there's one on it from the Chicken Shack!"

"Well, I'll be dipped. I think we've hit pay dirt!"

There were no lights on in the front of the house, so we decided to sneak around back and check for signs of life. Travis went to the right, and had to find his way through the bushes, and then climb over a fence. I went around to the left, where there was a sidewalk and a gate. We both made it to the back yard, but I had to wait a few minutes for him to show up.

The reflection of the moon on the surface of the lake helped us to see. We had stopped to admire the view, and to let Travis catch his breath, when I thought I heard a voice.

Up on the second level of the house, there was a sliding glass door that led out onto a small deck. We could see a dim light shining through it.

We both lowered our voices.

"Travis, I think there's someone up there."

"Hey, you said you brought your camera. You think you can get a picture?"

"I'm sure going to try."

I pointed my camera and pushed the button. It clicked, but that was it. I'd forgotten to put a flashcube on it!

Then we heard a second voice from the deck. That person started complaining about wasting a whole package of tobacco trying to roll a cigarette one-handed!

I put on a flashcube and aimed my camera in their direction. This time, it lit up the whole sky!

"Corky, let's get the hell out of here!"

"Go this way, Travis, there's a gate."

Travis took off running, but I slipped on something and fell down. I still had my camera in my hand, so I quickly snapped two more pictures. Then I got up and hauled ass out of there!

"Corky, what the hell were you doing?"

"I fell down!"

"Come on, let's get the flock out of here!"

Just then, the front door opened and Jimmy and Mary Ellen started yelling at us. We took off running, and then heard a gunshot! We jumped in the truck and I put the pedal to the floor! This time we really did smack our heads on the roof!

Neither one of us said much on the way back to town. We were too busy shaking in our boots. But as soon as we pulled into Bertha's parking lot, we started laughing.

"That was too cool, Corky!"

"Travis, I think I need a beer!"

"Well, partner, I'm buying. It's celebration time!"

"What's the occasion?"

"I've always wanted to be a detective, now I are one!"

Travis paid for the drinks, but it was all we could do to stop laughing long enough to even take the first sip. Then he got a squint-eyed look on his face and pointed to my pant leg, while pinching his nose.

"Corky, I hope you don't meet the love of your

life in here tonight."

I looked down at my pants. My right leg was all smeared with something, and as soon as I saw it, I smelled it, as well.

"Oh, shit!"

"Corky, I think you're on to something there."

"Travis, why didn't you tell me I was covered in muck?"

"I just now spotted it!"

"Great. Now what do I do?"

"Oh, heck, if anyone in here notices, say that you went to the North Pole."

"The North Pole? What the hell has that got to do with anything?"

"Just tell them you tripped over an elf, and fell in reindeer droppings!"

"I didn't go to the North Pole! We went to see Jimmy and Mary Ellen! Where do you come up with this North Pole crap?"

"Hey, stinky, you're the one coming up with the crap!"

"How come you didn't smell it in the truck?"

"How come you didn't?"

"I was too busy driving like a madman!"

"Well, maybe you should consider how the inside of your truck smells all the time!"

"Are you saying my truck smells like Rudolph's dung?"

"Hey, if the hoof fits!"

"Travis, I'm going home and take a hot shower,

and burn these clothes!"

"Okay, but watch out for those elves!"

I limped out to my truck, feeling lucky that the Buettemeier sisters didn't show up, after all!

Chapter Twenty-Four

After I left Bertha's, Travis decided to hang around till closing, because an opportunity had presented itself at the pool table.

A smart-mouthed young guy, with a few too many beers in him, kept referring to Travis as an old man. Travis ran the table a couple of times, and after shrinking down to the size of a wet spot on the floor, the young guy slammed his cue down and left. Unfortunately, they were the only two left in the place other than the help. Travis would have preferred an audience.

The next morning, Travis overslept and arrived at the barbershop a few minutes late. He got the door unlocked and had one foot inside when his phone started ringing. He figured it was probably someone calling for a sports interview about his professional pool playing abilities.

"Barbershop, Travis the pool shark speaking."

"Mr. O'Riley, this is Mary Ellen Smythe."

"Uh, hi there. What can I do for you, Mary Ellen?"

"You can meet me at the Bite Time today for lunch. We have things to talk about."

"I don't know if I can make it, Mary Ellen. I'm pretty busy."

"Be there at one o'clock, Travis."

She hung up and Travis spent the next few hours sweating. He was still edgy when I showed up.

"Hey, Mister Barber Man."

"We've got trouble, Corky."

"Now what?"

"Mary Ellen Smythe called this morning, and she wants me to meet her for lunch. She said we have things to discuss."

"What kind of things?"

"I don't know. That's all she said before hanging up."

"Well, it's been fun, Travis, but I've got a train to catch. See you later."

"Stay right where you are. You're in this up to your jewels, same as me. You're coming with."

"Gee, Travis, I'd really like to, but my cat is sick with diarrhea. I've got to go clean the carpet."

"Sit your ass down! We've got to figure out what we're going to say to her."

"Maybe it has nothing to do with last night."

"Corky, are you crazy?"

"Travis, don't go getting all worked up for nothing."

"If there's one thing I know about, Corky, it's haircuts and women. Trust me, she knows."

"Haircuts and women makes two things. You said there's one thing you know about."

"Corky, would you just stuff it!"

"Travis, here, take a look at these."

I took the photos from my shirt pocket and handed them to him.

"I thought you only took one picture. How did you wind up with three?"

"When I slipped and fell, I snapped a couple more."

"These are great! Can you believe what those two love birds are wearing?"

"Travis, check out Jimmy. All he's got on is a leopard-skin thong!"

"Yeah, but look at Mary Ellen! She's wearing a leather teddy! I like this shot where she's hanging over the railing."

"I thought the first one, where she's got herself wrapped around Jimmy, was the best."

"You know something, with these pictures, we've got Mary Ellen by the short hairs."

"That must be barber talk. You better explain."

"Whatever it is she wants, I'm betting one look at these, and she'll back off."

"Maybe we should offer to sell them to her,

kind of like a blackmail thing."

"Not a bad idea. Did you have any extra copies made, or are these three it?"

"When I got them developed, and saw what was there, I had the girl make me three sets. One for you, one for me, and a spare."

"Excellent! I couldn't have done better myself."

"Thanks, Mr. Detective."

"Corky, I sense that you're getting hungry."

"Well, looking at these pictures does make me kind of hungry for pie."

"Would that be hair pie?"

"How did you know?"

"The all-powerful barber can read minds!"

Travis and I headed across the street to the Bite Time Café. We got there a few minutes early, so we could try and get the drop on Mary Ellen. We didn't know if she would be alone or not, so we wanted to stack the cards in our favor as much as possible. We took a table in the very back, out of the mainstream.

Mary Ellen showed up a few minutes later, and Travis waved her over to where we were sitting. As she got closer, we could see that she wasn't her normal, cheerful self.

"Travis O'Riley, what's he doing here? This was supposed to be a meeting between you and me."

"I found Corky wandering the streets, and I offered to buy him a meal."

"Mr. O'Riley, I don't think I like this arrangement."

"Well, Ms. Smythe, whatever it is you have to say, Corky would likely hear from me, anyhow."

Sally came over to take our orders. I wanted a peanut butter and jelly sandwich with potato chips, and Travis ordered the day's special, as always. Mary Ellen just wanted coffee.

While we waited for our food, Travis and I made small talk about some of the other customers. We were just trying to keep things cool, and avoid a confrontation with Mary Ellen.

Our orders arrived a few minutes later, and I started eating my food immediately. The special of the day was fried pork patties in gravy, so Travis had to let his cool down a bit before digging in. Mary Ellen, on the other hand, dug into her purse and brought out a flask, then poured a shot in her coffee. Travis and I were sure surprised by that!

"O'Riley, I want to know what you two buttheads were doing snooping around my house last night?"

"Why, Mary Ellen, what in the world are you talking about?"

"Don't try to deny it, Travis. I have proof."

"Gee whiz, Mary Ellen. Corky and I spent the evening at Bertha's last night, discussing the number of elves that Santa employs at the North Pole."

"Travis, enough! My neighbor saw a pickup truck parked on our road when he was walking his dog. It had a handyman sign on the door."

"Oh, no! I forgot to take my magnetic signs off!"

"Calm down, Corky. Have another bite of your jelly roll."

"It's a sandwich, Travis. I only eat jelly rolls for breakfast."

"Whatever. Just keep eating."

"O'Riley, are you going to tell me what you and your sidekick were up to last night, or do I need to get the sheriff involved?"

"I don't think you really want Sheriff Drew involved. Your secret would be all over town if you brought him into this."

"My secret? I don't have any secrets!"

"Corky, would you show the lovely lady what's in your pocket."

It only took Mary Ellen a split second to realize the pictures were of her and Jimmy. Her face turned red, just like Travis's rear end did after he dropped his drawers in the poison ivy last summer.

"You still want to get the sheriff involved? We would have to show him the pictures. Then everybody in town would know that you've been messing around with an under-aged kid."

"He's not under-aged!"

"Three years ago he was!"

"What are you talking about?"

"Corky, why don't you tell Ms. Smythe about your new friend."

I started talking about making friends with Jimmy at Diamond Car Rentals, and then continued with the story about taking him to lunch and listening to his tales of an older woman. Mary Ellen slid further down in her chair with every word.

"Mary Ellen, Corky and I have been made to look like idiots by the sheriff. He's telling everyone that we reported a false crime. But, we know it's not false, and so do you. We also know that your lover boy Jimmy is involved in the disappearance of Nicky Torrelli. Make that one dead Nicky Torrelli."

"I have no idea what you're talking about, Travis."

"Mary Ellen, I got Leroy Lacome to spill the beans. He told me that he moved Torrelli's body on orders from Cousin Jimmy."

That was the straw that broke her. The tears started and she reached back in her purse for the flask.

Travis moved over and tried to put his arm around her, and that's when I noticed she had a hicky on her neck. She pushed Travis away and then began to speak.

"Two years ago, Mr. Palmer and Mr. Claymore brought Anita here from Chicago. Mr. Claymore met with Mayor Bartholomew and Sheriff Ledbetter, to fill them in on the situation. He wanted help keeping Anita's whereabouts a secret, so that Torrelli couldn't find her.

"Last month, Mr. Claymore received word from Chicago that Torrelli had been released from prison early, so he got everybody together again to talk about keeping the secret. Sheriff Ledbetter said he would personally take care of Torrelli if he ever showed up in Palmer Lake.

"A few days ago, I took a call from one of the guards at Palmer Industries. He was unable to reach the sheriff, so he called the mayor's office instead. He reported that a stranger had been causing trouble out at the plant. I told Mayor Bartholomew about the phone call, but he didn't seem too concerned.

"Later that day, when Sheriff Ledbetter showed up, I gave him the message, but he figured it was just another ex-employee who had been fired for drinking on the job.

"The next day, the guard called again. The stranger had come back. This time, the mayor seemed worried. He said if it was Torrelli, he didn't think Sheriff Ledbetter was man enough to handle the problem.

"That evening, when Jimmy came to visit, all I could do was talk about how Torrelli might be in town. After listening to my story, Jimmy told me he wanted to help and asked me to put him in touch with the guard at Palmer Industries.

"That's everything I know, Travis."

"I don't believe you, Mary Ellen. I think you know more."

"Travis, I'm telling the truth!"

"Mary Ellen, do you really expect me to believe that Jimmy didn't tell you what he did, after getting together with the guard?"

"Travis, I've asked him about it several times, but all he says is that he planted the problem."

"What the hell does that mean?"

"I don't know. Young people speak their own language, and sometimes it's hard to tell what they mean."

For some reason, listening to her talk about Jimmy made me picture an ugly girl going to a cheerleader tryout. She must have struck out with the guys during high school, and was making up for it now by hanging out with a teenager.

The more she talked, the more I kept flashing back to my teen years, remembering a time when I wanted to get it on with my neighbor, Nancy Bakersley. Nancy wouldn't give me the time of day, but her chubby, older sister Katie did. We only messed around once, though, because as soon as she got on top, I couldn't breathe and I blacked out.

Mary Ellen had finished her coffee, and now was taking straight shots from the flask. I kind of wanted to hang around and see if she would tip over, but something she said had got the wheels turning in my head.

"Hey, Travis, I've got to go meet a guy and look

at a plumbing job."

"What? Right now?"

"I told him I'd be there at two, and it's quarter till."

"Corky, we're right in the middle of something big here!"

"Travis, you're the one who wants to be a detective. Just keep at it."

I finished the last bite of my sandwich and then stood up. Mary Ellen had become so involved with her flask, she didn't even realize I was leaving.

Travis was just getting warmed up, and he decided to keep questioning her after I left.

"Mary Ellen, do you think Jimmy killed Nicky Torrelli?"

"Don't be ridiculous. I told him that Torrelli needed to be run out of town."

"What made you think Jimmy, of all people, could take care of that?"

"You're just a hairdresser. When Jimmy takes off his glasses, he's Superman."

"Mary Ellen, he's only nineteen!"

"He's more powerful than a daily planet, mister."

Ms. Smythe had emptied the flask, and gotten herself pretty medicated. Travis decided it was time to do something about the situation.

"Mary Ellen, I think it would be a good idea if I gave you a ride home. You can't go back to work shit-faced."

"What did you say about my face?"

"Come on, let's see if you can stand up."

Travis helped Mary Ellen get out of her chair, and then guided her to the door. From there, he led her across the street to the barbershop parking lot, and put her on the back of his motorcycle. Once underway, Travis had to drive a lot slower than he was used to, just so Mary Ellen wouldn't fall off.

When they finally arrived at her house, he had to help her off the motorcycle, and up the front steps. It took quite an effort by her to find the key to the door, but once they got inside, he had her sit down on the couch, and then he took the seat next to her.

Travis was just starting to ask Mary Ellen more questions about Jimmy, when she leaned over, put her head on his shoulder, and passed out.

Chapter Twenty-Five

When the three of us were at the restaurant, Mary Ellen mentioned that Jimmy had "planted the problem." For some reason, I couldn't seem to let that go, and the longer I sat there, the more it kept bugging me.

I didn't really have a plumbing job to go look at like I told Travis, but it made for a good excuse to leave. I went outside, jumped in my truck, and headed for Thomas Road.

When I arrived at the Palmers', Anita was in the front yard picking flowers. She saw me pull in, and stopped her gardening.

"Well, well, well. Look who's back. I suppose your truck needs water again?"

"No, but thanks for asking. I came to see Aaron. Is he here?"

"Since you're so smart, why don't you tell me?"

"I really need to talk to him, Anita. It's important."

"Why? Did you find another dead body on our property? Where was it this time, floating in the hot tub?"

"Anita, are you alright?"

"I'm fine! It's you that's screwed up! I think that spider bite medicine makes you hallucinate."

"You know, you're probably right. I was just noticing how beautiful you are, but it must be the drugs."

"Corky, you're a real creep! I called the sheriff after your last visit and told him all about you coming here and causing problems!"

"You're the one who did that?"

"And I'm not afraid to do it again!"

"Anita, go tell Aaron I'm here, and I'll wait in my truck like a good boy."

"You better not try anything, like driving into my fountain again!"

She strutted across the circular driveway with her arms waving, carrying on another conversation with the invisible man.

I sat in my truck listening to a Troublemakers album, and was kind of half asleep when Aaron appeared at my window.

"Corky, I've been told, in a rather unpleasant tone, that you want to see me again. What's on your mind?"

"Well, you wanted me to keep you updated about Nicky Torrelli."

"You have more information?"

"I think so."

"You think so? Corky, I've got a lot to do at my desk right now. What do you have for me?"

"How about you and me take another walk down to the barn."

"We've already done that once before, Corky."

"I think you'll understand better after I show you something."

"Let's make it quick. I just told a customer that I'd call him right back."

Aaron and I walked down to the barn. I was getting used to his quiet behavior, so this time it didn't bug me like it did before.

"Aaron, we're going to need a few things from in here."

"What are you talking about, Corky?"

"We'll need this garden shovel and that bucket, and we should probably take some gloves."

"What's all this for?"

"Just follow me and I'll show you."

"Can't you just tell me what this is about?"

"Aaron, if I'm wrong, I won't bother you anymore. But if I'm right, well, you'll see."

I put the shovel and the gloves in the bucket and we headed back up the gravel lane. When we had gone about three-quarters of the way, I stopped.

"Aaron, are you able to climb over this fence?"

"Why do you ask?"

"Because, if you're not, we can walk out to the road and go around."

"Corky, why do you want to go over to the Lacomes'?"

"Because. Now do we climb or do we walk?"

"What if they see us in their yard?"

"Don't worry, Mama and Leroy are both at work."

"Who is Mama?"

"Mama Lacome. Leroy's mother."

"Her name is Lottie."

"Maybe to you, but to everyone in town, she's known as Mama."

"You should show her some respect, Corky."

"And you should make up your mind."

"Oh, alright, let's climb the damn fence."

I went first so Aaron could hand me the bucket. Once he made it over, he crouched down and tried to be sneaky. It reminded me of watching an old black-and-white burglar flick. I grew up spying on the neighbor girls, peeking in their bedroom windows, so it all came natural to me.

We went around the backside of Leroy's garage, and stayed there for a minute so Aaron could catch his breath. Then we crossed the dirt driveway and made our way through the tall grass in their yard.

"Corky, you made me climb the fence and sneak around to show me this? I'm starting to think Anita is right - you are messed up on prescription medication!"

"Aaron, hand me the gloves and the shovel."
"Why?"
"Aaron, just give me the stuff!"

Aaron was getting to be a pain in the ass, just like his wife. Any normal guy would have given his left nut to be sneaking around on a secret mission like this. Just think of the stories that could be told at Bertha's!

"Aaron, hang on to the bucket, so I can put the flowers in it."

At first he hesitated, but then he did as instructed. I started digging up the plants, one at a time, and putting them in the bucket. I had to handle them carefully, because if my suspicions were wrong, I'd need to replant them.

I finally got all of them out, and now it was time to start digging down a little deeper. We only brought the little handheld garden shovel, so making progress was going to take time.

"Aaron, why don't you take over? Here's the shovel."

"Corky, it's one thing for me to be standing here watching you destroy the Lacomes' property, but I certainly didn't sign up to help."

I grabbed him by the arm and stuck the shovel in his hand.

"Aaron, you're the one who asked me to provide you with information about Nicky Torrelli. Now quit acting like a pussy, and start digging!"

That must have been the magic word, because

he started rolling up the sleeves of his white dress shirt.

"Where do I start?"

"How about in the middle?"

"Since the bucket is full, where should I put the dirt?"

"Just make a pile on the ground."

Aaron put on the gloves and started digging, while I snuck over to the fence to be our lookout.

As I was standing there keeping watch, I heard a noise. I turned around see where it came from, and saw Aaron, frozen in place, with one hand over his mouth.

He had dug a small hole about eight inches deep, and in the bottom of it I could see something shiny. I looked a little closer, and realized I was staring at a hand. The shiny thing was a big gold ring. My hunch was right - Torrelli's body was buried in the Lacomes' bathtub planter!

I started clearing away more dirt from around the hand. Aaron had made his way over to the fence, and was hanging on as best he could. Then came that unmistakable sound.

I stopped what I was doing and went to see if I could help. Aaron had gotten sick, and he smelled even worse than the manure pile at the barn.

"I've got to call the sheriff, Corky. Can you help me get over the fence?"

"Why don't we walk around? You're in no shape to be climbing anything."

"But I have to call him right now!"

"Aaron, come on. It will only take a minute to go around."

"No, Corky! I have to climb the fence!"

He stood up very slowly, put one foot on the bottom rail, and began to climb. It reminded me of the time I watched a slug crawl over a dog turd.

When he finally made it to the other side, I followed. Then the two of us walked around the circular driveway to the house, and went inside.

Anita was in the entryway straightening the skinny dippers picture, and when she saw us come through the front door, she immediately threw a fit.

"Aaron, what's he doing in here? I don't want him in our house!"

"Anita, could you get me the phone, please."

"All he does is cause trouble!"

"Go get me the phone, Anita."

"Ever since he was in here, this picture has been hanging crooked, and I can't get it to hang straight! What did you do to it, Corky?"

"Did you hear me, Anita? Get me the phone!"

"Look at the dirt on his boots! You get outside with the other animals, Corky!"

"Anita, I have to call the sheriff! We just discovered a body at the Lacomes'!"

"Oh boy! Here we go again with the dead body thing! Isn't that story getting a bit old?"

"The phone, Anita!"

"Aaron, you should know better than to go to the Lacomes'. You stink! That place is filthy!"

Aaron gave up and left the room. I just stood there, not knowing what to do.

"I told you to get, Corky! You're as dirty as the Slyfields' hogs!"

The Slyfields' hogs? I didn't need to be told that story again! I went outside, got in my truck, and rolled a smoke.

Chapter Twenty-Six

I sat in my truck trying to sort out all the details of the Torrelli mystery, while staying out of Anita's line of fire. I couldn't help but think that Leroy must have had more to do with it than what he told Travis.

Oh, shit! Travis! I needed to call him and let him know we found the body! I jumped out and was headed for the front porch, when the door opened and out came Aaron. I put on the brakes, and waited to see if Anita was coming out to chase me off with her broom. Fortunately, Aaron was alone.

"Corky, I called the sheriff's office, but Drew wasn't there. I left word for him to call me as soon as he gets the message."

"Aaron, I need to make a call, too. Any chance of using your phone?"

"I wouldn't go in the house, Corky. Anita is so

mad about the picture, her eyes are crossed. I've only seen that happen once before, when I had the putting green installed. There's a phone in the garage you can use, but make it quick. I don't want the sheriff to get a busy signal."

We walked past the peeing boy fountain and went over to the garage. There was an entry around the side where we could get in, but it was so dark in there, I waited in the doorway for Aaron to turn on the lights.

The place looked like the showroom at a new car dealership. It was big enough to hold four cars, plus lots of extra room for other stuff. The floor was painted where the cars parked, and the rest of the place was carpeted in red and gray squares.

Aaron led me over to an area that looked a lot like a kitchen. There were cabinets, countertops, and a sink, and along the wall were six vending machines! The telephone was mounted next to the paper towel holder, and I grabbed it and called Travis.

"Barbershop, please hold."

"Travis! It's Corky! Travis?"

Crap! He put the phone down! I could hear him in the background using the cash register, and telling someone about a girl he used to take camping.

"This is your friendly forest ranger, Travis."

"Travis, it's Corky. I've got to talk fast, so just listen."

"Corky? Are you back from looking at that plumbing job?"

"Travis, listen to me! I'm at the Palmers' house, and you need to get out here right now! Torrelli's body turned up!"

"No kidding?"

"Hop on your motorcycle and get moving! I want you here when the sheriff shows up."

"Is he on his way?"

"Aaron left a message for him, and we're waiting for him to call back."

"Corky, I could peddle a tricycle and beat Drew."

"Listen, I've got to get off the phone. Just get out here!"

I sat down on one of the designer stools to catch my breath. I hadn't been that excited since I first discovered the body in the blackberries!

"Aaron, do you smoke?"

"No."

"I'm surprised, living with Anita."

"I keep a bottle in my office."

"I need a cigarette. You want one? It might help you relax."

"Corky, I've got to stay by the phone."

"Oh, that's right."

"You go ahead. Just don't let her catch you. You'll never hear the end of it."

"Aaron, it doesn't matter what I do around here, I never hear the end of it!"

"Tell me about it."

"Okay, I'll be in my truck. Let me know when

the sheriff calls back. I can't wait to hear what he has to say."

I figured it would be a while, so I turned on the music and sat on the floor of my truck smoking a cigarette. It wasn't comfortable, but it was better than being caught by Anita!

After twenty minutes or so, my behind was getting pretty sore, and I'd heard all of side one on the tape. I got out of the truck and went back to the garage. Aaron was just finishing up on the phone.

"Corky, the sheriff wouldn't believe my story about finding a body in the planter!"

"That sounds familiar."

"And when I mentioned your name, he started laughing at me! I had to threaten having him fired before he would take me seriously!"

"So, is he coming, or not?"

"He told me he would be here after he finished his lunch."

"Well, if he's eating, we might not see him for a while. Drew's kind of a pig."

"No kidding! When he came to our Christmas party last year, he grabbed the plate with the sausages on it, then sat down by himself and ate all of them! No one else got any!"

"He was probably having grease withdrawals. Aaron, you thought anymore about having a smoke?"

"Oh, what the hell."

"Maybe we should go around the back of the

house, so we're out of sight."

"Oh, that's right. I almost forgot about Anita."

"I find that hard to believe!"

I pulled out my tobacco and rolled a couple cigarettes. Aaron's eyes about popped out of their sockets.

"How on earth did you learn to do that? They look just like real cigarettes."

"They are real cigarettes."

"No, I mean they look like they are store bought."

"Here, take the matches."

Aaron lit up and immediately started coughing. It reminded me of some of my friends back in junior high. He only made it halfway through his before putting it out.

He was telling me the story about Anita's addiction to vending machines when we were interrupted by the sound of a motorcycle. We went around front, and there was Travis. He appeared to be having trouble with his kickstand.

"Corky, I don't know what's wrong with this damn thing."

"If I was you, Travis, I'd be more concerned about the oil stains on my pants than a broken kickstand."

"Where the hell did all that come from?"

"Looks like your side cover is leaking."

"Crap!"

"Just be glad you didn't have one of your girlfriends on the back. She'd be soaked!"

"Oh, great. I gave Mary Ellen a ride home from the Bite Time because she was too sloshed to drive."

"Well, when she sobers up and sees her pants, she'll be wondering what kind of a ride you really gave her!"

Aaron was hanging around, keeping quiet as usual, so I decided to introduce him to Travis.

"Aaron, this is my friend, Travis O'Riley. He's the other half of the investigation team."

"You look familiar, Travis. Have we met?"

"I've seen you in my barbershop once or twice. You should drop in again. I can fix that problem you're having with your hair."

I'd heard Travis use that line a million times, and it never failed to make guys wonder. I thought it was an ingenious way to build business.

"Hey, you two, I think I hear a siren."

"I think you're right, Aaron. Must be our fearless sheriff. It's only taken him, what, two hours since you first left the message?"

"Pretty close to that."

Drew's patrol car sped into the circular driveway and came to a screeching stop in front of us. He got out and immediately started shouting orders at Travis and me.

"You two stay right where you are! This is an official police matter."

TROUBLE COMES TO PALMER LAKE

"Drew, leave them alone, they're my guests. Let's go inside and get this situation under control."

Travis and I decided to go wait in my truck. As we turned and headed in that direction, I thought I saw something moving out of the corner of my eye. Sure enough, Anita was on the porch, glaring at all of us.

Aaron and Drew were heading toward the house, when Aaron spotted Anita and called to her. She turned and stormed back inside, slamming the front door so hard that one of the porch lights fell, shattering glass all over the concrete!

"Travis, did you see that?"

"What just happened, Corky?"

"Anita has been heating up ever since I arrived. I think she just boiled over!"

Aaron and Drew hurried to the front porch. Then we heard another crash. The sheriff slipped on the broken glass and smashed into a wooden bench!

"Travis, the sheriff just fell on his ass!"

"Good thing he's got plenty of bacon fat back there. His ass just saved his life!"

Aaron helped Drew get back on his feet, and the two of them went inside.

"Travis, I'll bet the climate in that house is pretty frigid!"

"Corky, speaking of frigid, you think I could use their bathroom?"

"Get serious!"

"But I've really gotta go!"

"Just use the backseat of the patrol car. Drew won't mind."

Travis apparently didn't like my suggestion. He chose to water down Drew's rear tire instead.

Chapter Twenty-Seven

Travis and I sat in my truck talking about Mary Ellen and Jimmy while waiting for Aaron and Drew to come back outside. They finally appeared about a half-hour later. We climbed out of the truck, and the sheriff confronted us once again.

"You two get back in the truck and stay there!"

"Drew, back off! Corky, you didn't happen to see Anita come out here, did you?"

"No. We haven't seen anyone come out except you two. Why?"

"After I finished telling about digging up the body, she left the room in tears. The sheriff wanted me to stay put until he finished his phone call to the Lacomes, and by that time, she was nowhere to be found."

"It's a big house. Maybe she's hiding in a closet?"

"I doubt that. I think she must have gone out the back door and down to the barn."

Travis had been standing there listening, until something rubbed him the wrong way and he butted in.

"Aaron, the sheriff wouldn't let you be with your wife, even though she was crying?"

"Well, no."

"Drew, somebody ought to teach you some manners!"

The sheriff took a few steps backwards, and bumped up against his patrol car's wet tire. Then he got a serious look on his face.

"Aaron, I need to take a look at the body so I can file my report."

"Sheriff, you just told me that you were going to wait for the Lacomes to get home before going over there."

"I've changed my mind."

The two of them headed for the Lacomes', with Aaron in the lead. Since they weren't going to climb the fence, the walk would take them a few minutes, as slow as Drew moved. Travis and I noticed the back of his pant leg was wet, and we started laughing.

"Come on, Travis! Let's go jump the fence!"

"Now you're talking! Let's hit it!"

We ran across the driveway, and both of us had one foot up on the bottom rail, when suddenly we stopped our climb.

"Travis, do you see who I see?"

"Would that be Mrs. Palmer?"

"That's her, alright. There's no mistaking Anita!"

"What the hell is she doing?"

"It looks like she's removing dirt from the bathtub with her hands!"

"Corky, it sounds like she's carrying on a conversation."

"Come on Travis, let's check it out."

We got over the fence and headed for the planter. Just as we did, we heard the sound of the Lacomes' car pulling in.

"Travis, let's hurry. Leroy and Mama just got home."

When we got to the planter, Anita had uncovered Torrelli's face, and was talking to him. She seemed to be in another world, and wasn't even aware that we were there.

"I'm sorry I got mad when you came to see me, Nicky. I was worried that Aaron would find out you were here, and I didn't want him to know out about our plans. Can you forgive me?"

Travis started whispering to me.

"Corky, what the hell do you make of that?"

"Sounds like she was up to no good. Let's keep quiet so we can hear more."

"You know I love you, Nicky. I've always loved you. I'll save you, just like I did before."

"Corky, this is getting pretty weird. How's she

going to save him? Doesn't she know he's dead?"

"Travis, if you'd seen all the screwy stuff that I've seen go on with her, you'd think this was perfectly normal. She has conversations with invisible people every time I'm here!"

"No kidding?"

"She reminds me of a girl in the neighborhood where I grew up, named Candy Cluster. Candy got a pimple on her ass and went around showing it to all us kids, telling us it was her cherry, and that her mom was going to pop it when it got bigger."

"Corky, where do you dream up this stuff? Her mom was going to pop her cherry? That was your job, you idiot!"

"I'm not kidding! We were all flying kites in the field next to her house when she showed us!"

"So, did Anita show you her ass? Or was it her cherry?"

"Thanks, Travis! Neither one!"

"Hey, Corky, cut it short. Here come the four stooges."

"Now we're busted!"

Walking single file through the un-mown front yard came Aaron and Sheriff Ledbutt, followed by Leroy and Mama. Drew spotted us and started right in.

"I told you two this is official police business and to stay in the truck! Now I'm going to have to treat you as criminals!"

Travis stepped in front of Drew, and put his

face an inch from his.

"You listen to me, fat boy! You're a lazy, good-for-nothing, sack of decomposed possum shit! You think you're so high and mighty cause you wear a badge! How'd you like me to pin it on your ass, where it belongs? Then you'd really have some explaining to do when your mommy changes your diaper!"

Now we'd be going to jail for sure! What was Travis thinking? But it didn't stop there!

"We were the ones who told you about the dead guy in the first place! You accused us of making it up, and told the whole town we're a couple of screw-ups! And since you'd rather sit on your bacon-butt and fish, Corky did the investigating, and located the missing body! You even try taking credit for solving this, and I'll make sure the whole town knows you still wet the bed!"

Travis turned around and walked back over by me. Sheriff Drew looked like he was going to burst into flames! During all of this, Anita was still talking to Nicky, and never even knew it took place!

Then, Mama Lacome took a turn.

"Sheriff, you're not the only one, you know. Leroy still has accidents and potties his bed, too. That's why I don't like him to drink."

I'd never seen a man shrink like that before. Drew must have lost five or six inches in height. Travis may have started it, but Mama Lacome definitely finished it!

Drew avoided eye contact with all of us, and inched his way over to the tub to have a look at the body.

"Aaron, come get your wife. I need to get in here for a closer look."

Aaron went over to bathtub and put his arm around Anita. Bad move! She came out of her other world and went off like a firecracker!

"It should be you and your golf clubs in here, Aaron Palmer!"

Aaron quickly let go of her and stepped back.

"I've been miserable living here! I wanted to stay in Chicago and wait for Nicky to get out, so we could get married!"

Then it was Leroy's turn. He went over and stood next to her.

"Miss Anita, I didn't kill him, I just moved him from the woods to my garage like Jimmy told me to. I didn't want you to get in trouble for having a dead body on your property. I like you a lot, Miss Anita."

"Leroy Lacome, you get away from that woman and come stand next to your mama!"

Mama Lacome had put her foot down, and Leroy immediately did as he was told.

Sheriff Drew was trying to get a look at the body, but wasn't any closer to accomplishing his mission. So, he went to the opposite side of the tub and peered in.

"I need to go radio for help. All of you just stay here."

TROUBLE COMES TO PALMER LAKE

The sheriff started to head for the road, but then stopped and handcuffed Leroy!

"You're coming with me, Leroy Lacome. You're under arrest for murder!"

"You leave my boy alone! He's not going anywhere!"

"Mrs. Lacome, this is official police business. You stay out of my way, or I'll have to arrest you for interfering!"

"You heard what he said to that Palmer woman! He just moved the body!"

Mama Lacome kicked dirt at Drew, then stuck out her tongue and flipped him off. But that didn't stop him. He walked Leroy over to the Palmers', and put him in the back of his patrol car.

"Corky, I need a drink!"

"Travis, I need a smoke!"

The two of us climbed back over the fence, and headed for my truck.

Chapter Twenty-Eight

Travis and I were walking across the circular driveway, headed for my truck, when Drew spotted us, and slid out of the patrol car like a greased pig.

"Okay, you two, hold it right there! What do you think you're up to?"

"Sheriff, Travis and I are taking a break."

"You two better not get any ideas, like leaving the scene of the crime!"

"The thought never crossed my mind, Sheriff. How about yours, Travis?"

"It did cross my mind, Corky."

"You two get in the truck and stay put. The county police are on their way, and they want to talk to the both of you."

"Sheriff, are you going to leave Leroy handcuffed in the backseat of your car until they get here?"

"Perkins, he's a criminal! He stays right where he is!"

"Sheriff, aren't you concerned about his weak bladder?"

That made Drew stop for a second, and he got a concerned look on his face. But then, he turned and headed back to the Lacomes'.

"Hey, Travis, didn't we come back to the truck to smoke and drink?"

"Drinking was my intention."

"Well, then, let's get started."

"Corky, did you see Drew's face when you mentioned Leroy's bladder?"

"Yeah. He's probably thinking about his own. I'll bet all this excitement's got him ready to burst!"

"You know, I'm about due myself."

"Travis, you just watered the patrol car, not even an hour ago!"

"Oh, that's right. I guess staring at that peeing boy fountain over there makes me think about it."

I put on the Troublemakers' Christmas album, just as Travis was taking the first swig from his flask.

"Corky, you realize it's the middle of summer, don't you?"

"Sure, I know that."

"Then why are we listening to Log Cabin Christmas?"

"I figured it would fit in with all the other

strange stuff that's going on."

"It has been a day, hasn't it?"

"Travis, how did the two of us ever wind up living in such a screw-ball little town? I think we're the only sane people in Palmer Lake."

"Bertha's okay."

"That's true. I guess there are three of us, then."

"That should make you feel better."

"You know what would really make me feel better?"

"Probably rolling up a smoke. You seem to have forgotten that's what you came to do."

"I was thinking more along the lines of doing something to help poor Leroy. Remember when you picked the lock on Torrelli's satchel at your shop? Do you think you could do it on a pair of handcuffs?"

"What about Drew? He'd really have reason to shoot first and ask questions later, then."

"I'm not talking about turning him loose. Just let him out so he can drain his tank."

"That would be a decent thing to do."

"So, you'll give it a go?"

"Let me take a couple of swigs first. I need a little confidence."

"Well, while you're getting your confidence, I'll get my toolbox."

When Travis went over to the patrol car, he found that it wasn't locked. He opened the back door, and there was Leroy, lying on the seat all curled up and moaning.

"Hey, Leroy, it's me, Travis."

"Why are you here?"

"Corky thought you might need to drain your vein."

"How did he know?"

"Woman's intuition, Leroy."

"I've heard of that. What's it mean?"

"It means get out of the car, before you piss your pants!"

"But I'm in handcuffs, Travis!"

Travis helped Leroy out of the car, and told him to just stand there like he was waiting for a bus. Then he went around behind him and started messing with the cuffs.

"Corky, do you have any lubricant and a small nail?"

"Travis, I left my lubricant with the neighbor's wife. She didn't think my nail was small."

"Smart ass."

"How about some motor oil. Will that do?"

"That should work."

"Okay, I'll be right back."

"Corky, where are you going?"

"Just give me a minute."

I went over to his motorcycle, and sure enough, there was quite a puddle of oil under it on the driveway. I dipped a small nail in it that I'd taken from my toolbox, and brought it back to Travis.

"Will this work?"

"Corky, you're pretty amazing."

"Hey, that's what she said!"

"She? Who?"

"The neighbor's wife!"

"Oh, brother! Corky, just keep an eye out in case someone's coming."

It took Travis about a minute to unlock the cuffs. That was twice as long as it took him to unlock Nicky's satchel. But Leroy was thrilled!

"Okay, Leroy, go drain your tank in the peeing boy fountain, and then hurry your ass back here!"

"Travis, I'm not going to pee in Miss Anita's fountain!"

"Well, then go around the other side of the patrol car and piss on the tire. Just hurry it up!"

"I like that idea!"

Leroy went around the car to take care of business, while Travis and I stood guard.

"Hey, you guys, this tire is already wet!"

"Corky saw a dog here earlier."

"It must have been a big one. The tire is wet, all the way up on top!"

Leroy finished his business, and came right back. Now he was wearing his usual smile.

"I want to thank you guys for that. I was really hurting!"

"Leroy, it was Corky's idea. Thank him."

"Thanks, Corky. What a relief!"

"Hey, Travis, I've got an idea! You want to make

Sheriff Ledbutt think he's really losing his grip?"

"What are you talking about, Corky?"

"Put the cuffs back on Leroy, but stick him in the front seat just for fun. Then Drew will be the one wetting his pants!"

"That's a great idea! Leroy, you game?"

"Sure! I'm already in trouble with that stupid sheriff. A little more won't hurt none."

Travis put the cuffs back on him. Then they went around to the other side of the patrol car, and Leroy climbed in the front passenger's seat.

"I sure wish Mama could see me!"

"Leroy, we have to get back in the truck, before Ledbutt waddles back over here and catches us."

"Thanks again, you two."

Travis and I got in, and picked up where we left off. I rolled up that smoke I wanted, and he cracked open his flask. I had to put on different music though, because Travis kept complaining that the sound of jingle bells reminded him of a jailer's keys.

Chapter Twenty-Nine

When the county reinforcements arrived, it reminded me of the time that Bertha held a surprise get-together for unwed mothers one Saturday night. We counted nine police cars and a medical examiner's van.

Travis and I stayed in the truck watching as the cops all grouped together for a brief powwow before heading into the Lacomes' place. Then we decided to go watch the action from the fence.

The first officer to approach the bathtub was a female. She moved cautiously, because Anita was still hovering over Nicky. The lady cop spent a few minutes talking to her, and then was able to lead her away from the tub.

As soon as the coast was clear, two guys dressed in white moved in to check out the body. After ten minutes or so, they tried lifting Torrelli out of his dirt bath. They were having trouble, so two of the

TROUBLE COMES TO PALMER LAKE

cops came to help. That did the trick. Out from the planter came Nicky.

The four of them tipped him sideways, dumping off a bunch of dirt, and then put him on the stretcher. Then the guys in white wheeled him away to the van.

In the meantime, another one of the officers had been talking to Mama Lacome. She began ranting and raving about her boy not killing anyone, and the cop wasted no time signaling for help. Two more officers came to the rescue and helped escort Mama to her house.

Aaron started talking to one of the other cops, and the remaining officers all crowded around Sheriff Ledbutt. We could see Drew beaming.

"Corky, do you see how old fat-butt is puffing up his sunken chest in front of those guys?"

"Probably the first time he's ever had an audience."

"Well, it won't take long before they find out that he's full of hot air!"

"You think he's going to cut the cheese?"

"Corky, you idiot, that's not what I meant. Although, now that you mention it."

"Hey, look, Travis, the party's breaking up. I'll bet anything he let one rip!"

"Come on, Corky, we'd better get back to the truck before stinky spots us."

Travis and I hustled back to the truck, stopping just for a second to check on Leroy. He was still sitting in the front seat of Drew's patrol car, laughing.

We fired up the music once more and waited to see what would happen next. It didn't take long before we saw the lady cop walking Anita across the driveway. She led her to the front door and then took her inside. Aaron followed at a distance, along with one of the other officers, but the two of them stayed outside.

Soon after, Sheriff Drew and one of the county cops came over to talk with us.

"Here they are, Officer. Our town criminals. That one is Travis O'Riley and this is Corky Perkins. I blocked them in with my cruiser so they couldn't escape."

"Let me have a few minutes alone with these law-breakers, Sheriff. We have ways of getting these dangerous types to confess."

"Okay. I need to go check on my prisoner, anyhow."

"Say, Sheriff, county rules prohibit us from putting our prisoners in the front seat. Being a lone wolf, it must be different for you."

"What are you talking about?"

"I just noticed that your guy is up front."

"What the hell? How did he get up there? I handcuffed him and put him in the back seat!"

Drew hurried over to his car. We'd never seen him move that fast!

"You two wouldn't happen to know anything

about that, would you?"

I'm sure the county cop figured we had something to do with Leroy being in the front seat, but he seemed pretty amused by it.

"Corky, the sheriff said he blocked your truck in so you couldn't leave. Looks to me like there's plenty of room to get by him if you wanted to."

"Officer, I don't know how well you county guys know Drew, but people in Palmer Lake think he's one pickle short of a full jar."

"I'm beginning to understand. Hold on a minute, I'll be right back."

The officer walked over to the patrol car as Drew was returning Leroy to the back seat.

"Sheriff, everything under control here?"

"It was those two!"

"Sheriff, I see that your rear tire is all wet. You should have that checked. You might be leaking brake fluid."

The county cop came back over to my truck, shaking his head. It was easy to see that Drew had worked his magic on him, like he does on all of us.

"That guy is a real nut job."

"Officer, you don't know the half of it. Travis scared him so bad a little earlier, we're pretty sure he wet his pants."

"I thought I smelled urine just now."

"Trust me, Officer, I fix toilets for a living and I know the aroma. Most days, Drew smells like he uses it for after shave."

That did it. The county cop started laughing so hard that tears rolled down his cheeks.

"Listen, you two, I've got to transfer the sheriff's prisoner to one of our cars. Would you guys hang around a while? I need to get your statements."

"Good luck getting old Ledbutt to turn him over to you."

"Travis is right, Officer. Drew thinks he's the Lone Ranger."

The cop went back over to the Lacomes' and rounded up some help. A few minutes later, two county police cars pulled into the Palmers' driveway and blocked Drew in. It didn't take long before Leroy was transferred to one of their vehicles.

The Palmers' front door opened and out came Anita, followed by the policewoman carrying a suitcase. She led Anita to the other county cop car and put her in the backseat. Then both cars, the one with Leroy, and the one with Anita, pulled out and left. After that, Aaron and the officer who had escorted him went inside the house.

Our guy was headed back over to see us, and following right behind him was Sheriff Drew.

"Sheriff, this is county police business now. I'd appreciate it if you would leave us alone so I can take statements from these two gentlemen."

"Gentlemen? Those two are criminals and they need to be locked up!"

"Well, Sheriff, we'll see about that. For now,

please leave us alone."

"They killed that guy and made Leroy bury him in the bathtub!"

"Okay, Sheriff, thanks for your opinion. I'll take it from here."

"They let my prisoner out of the patrol car and put him in the front seat!"

"Sheriff Ledbetter, go take a walk."

"Those two are behind all of this!"

"Sheriff, get lost!"

Drew finally gave up. To make things even better, he got back in his car and left. What a relief!

"Okay, you guys, let's see if we can make this quick, so you can be on your way. Corky, why don't you tell me what your involvement in this whole thing was."

"Well, Officer, I was hired to work on the Palmers' barn. After I'd been there a couple of days, I started smelling something foul, so I went looking for the source of the stench, and wound up finding a dead guy in the woods. I went back to town for help, and the first person I found was Travis. He came back with me to see the body, and it turned out that he recognized the guy."

"Travis, you knew the victim?"

"He'd been in my barbershop a few days earlier, and I immediately recognized the quality of the haircut."

"Did you guys notify the sheriff?"

"Travis and I went back to town, but we didn't

locate him until the next morning."

"That's right, Officer. Corky and I spotted him pulling into the Bite Time Café, and we went to tell him about the dead guy. He didn't believe a word we said, so I had to get tough with him. When he finally got off his lazy ass, that's when things went from bad to crappy."

"What do you mean?"

"We drove back out here to show Drew the body, but it was gone. That's when he started threatening us."

"What kind of threats?"

"He said that we had reported a phony crime and he was going to lock us up."

"He didn't put you two in jail, did he?"

"No, he didn't. He decided to spread the word that Corky and I couldn't be trusted. I heard about it from customers in my barbershop!"

"So, the body turns up next door in the bathtub planter. Corky, Aaron Palmer said it was you that discovered it. How did that happen?"

"Well, since Drew wouldn't believe I found a body in the woods, Travis and I decided to start an investigation of our own. One thing led to another, and I acted on a hunch."

"That sounds more like something you'd read in a paperback mystery, Corky."

"Funny you should say that. I was going to suggest to Travis that we give some thought to writing a book about our adventure."

"Well, you might want to hold off on that until this thing gets resolved. Travis, do you have anything to add to this report?"

"Are you putting anything in there about Drew sticking Leroy in his front seat?"

"I made note of that. Why?"

"Oh, I just wanted to make sure that the whole county knows what a dumb shit he is, not just the people in Palmer Lake."

"I think I've got everything I need, except your phone numbers."

"I don't have a home phone, Officer. Should I put my barbershop number down instead?"

"That'll be fine, Travis."

"You should stop by my shop. I can fix that problem you're having with your haircut."

The officer thanked us, and then headed for the Lacomes', while trying to smooth his hair down. One by one, all of the county cops left the scene.

Chapter Thirty

Travis and I were finally able to get out of the truck and stretch our legs. I had to stretch more than that, so I went over to the fountain and imitated the peeing boy. Travis went to his motorcycle, and found the large puddle of oil on the driveway.

"Corky, did you see this? My motorcycle looks like it bled out!"

"Yeah, I saw it when I dipped the nail in it."

"Have you got any motor oil with you?"

"No. I told you I left my lubricant with the neighbor's wife."

"Smart ass. What the hell am I going to do?"

"Hey, Travis, I'll bet we could find some oil in Leroy's garage."

"I don't think we should go back over there, Corky."

"Why not? The cops are gone."

"Yeah, but Mama Lacome is still around."

"Come on, Travis. You just stood up to the sheriff! Don't tell me you're afraid of Mama Lacome?"

That little reminder was all it took. Travis and I climbed the fence and snuck over to the garage. Sure enough, there were cans of motor oil everywhere.

"Corky, Leroy must drink this stuff for breakfast! No wonder he looks like he does."

"Hey, Travis, this must be the station wagon that Leroy used to haul Torrelli's body in. You want to have a peek inside, just for fun?"

"We better just grab the oil and get the hell out of here, before Mama spots us."

"Maybe there's more evidence in it!"

"Don't you mean more grease?"

"Come on! Let's take a look!"

"Corky, the guy uses mattresses for working on cars. That's not normal, if you get my drift."

"Travis, did you have to say that? It makes me think about Debra and Lorraine."

"Corky, you need to forget about Lorraine. I heard a rumor that those two have been seen dancing together in Keselburg."

"They let girls dance with each other there?"

"I guess."

The back of Leroy's station wagon was open, so I took a look inside. The seat was folded down to make room for carrying stuff like bodies, and the thing was filthy!

"Hey, Travis, come here."

"Now, what?"

"Look over there by the edge of the passenger's door. You see that?"

"Yeah."

"What do you think it is?"

"It's probably just one of Leroy's rags."

"Why don't you go open the door and check?"

Travis went around the side of the car. He untucked his shirt and used it like a glove, so he wouldn't leave any fingerprints. Then he opened the door. When he did, whatever it was fell out.

"You better not touch that, Travis. Leroy probably blew his nose on it!"

"Corky, it's not one of his rags."

"What is it?"

"It's a payday."

"A candy bar?"

"No, you idiot. It's Mr. Chicago's bankroll!"

"His wad of bills? Let me see!"

"It must have slipped out of his pocket when he was being drug from the car."

We stood there gazing for a moment, and then Travis decided to count it. There were forty-six, one hundred-dollar bills. He divided it into two stacks of twenty-three each, and handed me one.

Travis grabbed a can of oil, and we very quietly climbed back over the fence. Once he was done refilling his motorcycle, we couldn't wait to go celebrate at Bertha's!

Chapter Thirty-One

When we pulled in the parking lot, I spotted Billy, Pinkie, and Rosie passing around a cigarette. I could only imagine what those three were smoking, after what Travis told me. I wasn't nearly so interested in those two girls as I had been.

Inside, Travis suggested we shoot some pool and relax. I wasn't much of a player, so I told him there would be no betting on the games. I'd be doing well just to know where my balls were.

"Travis, why do you think the cops hauled Anita off like that?"

"Because, she's only got one oar in the boat."

"Don't you mean in the water?"

"Not in her case!"

"What do you think they'll do with her?"

"The cops will dump her at the hospital."

"The hospital?"

"Yeah. Then they'll stick her in a little room,

and give her a coloring book and a couple of jigsaw puzzles, before sending her to counseling."

"Travis, get serious."

"Corky, have you ever spent any time with a shrink? Back when I was young, they made me go see one after I stole that cop's motorcycle."

"That's weird."

"Weird isn't the word for it. The lady shrink told me I stole the motorcycle because my mother didn't breast feed me!"

"Is that why you drink so much now?"

"Corky, shut up and take your shot."

It was always fun to see Travis get worked up like that. I tried to get his goat at least once a day.

"Travis, do you think anyone will know we took the money?"

"Corky, I don't think anyone knows it was there. If Leroy or Cousin Jimmy had seen it, it sure as hell wouldn't have been laying there for us to find! Anyhow, we deserve to get paid for all the work we did."

"What are you going to do with your half?"

"I'm going to live it up. How about you?"

"I could use some more tools."

"I figured you'd say something like that. Don't you want to spend some of it having fun, rather than on work?"

"What kind of fun?"

"Women and booze! What else?"

"I like the tool idea better."

"Corky, what am I going to do with you?"

"Travis, you're the drinker. And you're also the guy who has a gal waiting to fix you dinner. I'm the guy who fixes toilets and finds dead bodies!"

"Corky, some day you're going to be too old to enjoy women, and the doctor will tell you to quit drinking. You'd better do it while you can."

"Yeah, but between the Buettemeier sisters, and Lorraine, my choice of women is on a downhill slide. Besides, it might be a good idea if we sat on the money for a while. We don't want anyone getting suspicious."

"It's only twenty-three hundred each, Corky."

"But this is Palmer Lake. If people catch wind that we're throwing money around, they'll be talking. I think we should hide it under our mattresses. Anyhow, Travis, you need to spend some of it on that leaking motorcycle of yours, not on some leaking floozy."

"Damn, I forgot about my oil leak! You're right, I need to take care of that."

Travis and I played a couple more games of pool, which he naturally won, and then we decided to go get some dinner at the Bite Time.

On our way out, we spotted Billy Hamrod sitting on the hood of his car. His radio was turned way up and the Buettemeier girls were doing an erotic dance for him. I was only a little jealous.

Chapter Thirty-Two

Travis and I went to dinner, but it turned out I was so tired, I couldn't even finish all of my meal. I needed to go home and get some sleep. Spending the day in Corn Hole County really wore me out.

The next morning, it was all I could do to get out of bed by ten. I drug myself into the shower to remove the assortment of fragrances I'd brought home, such as horse manure, grave dirt, and the beer I spilled down the front of me at Bertha's after Travis sunk two pool balls in one shot.

I'd finally gotten dressed and was in the kitchen deciding what to have for breakfast, when my phone rang.

"Corky?"

"Travis, is that you?"

"Corky, I just got a surprise visit from our friend, the county cop."

"He came to get his haircut already? You must be a better salesman than you thought!"

"He didn't come for a haircut. He came to talk to me about the body. The medical report came back on Nicky Boy, and it says he died of heart failure."

"The guy had a heart attack?"

"Yes and no. His heart stopped because he was electrocuted!"

"Travis, I've heard stories about guys dying from pissing on an electric fence. Do they think Anita's fence did him in?"

"The cop didn't say anything about a fence. He told me they found burns on Torrelli's ass!"

"Travis, come on! I'm too tired to laugh at one of your lame jokes right now. Try it out on Toot."

"Since when are my jokes lame? You damn near crapped your pants last night when I told you the one about the girl with the feather duster!"

"That was pretty good. Okay, I take it back. So, did the cop say anything else?"

"He said the lab guys are out at the Lacomes', investigating."

"Why? Do they think Mama went after him with her electric cattle prod? I thought she only used that on Leroy!"

"He didn't say what they're looking for."

Just then, my doorbell rang.

"Hey, Travis, there's someone at my door. I'll have to call you back."

"It's probably the girl with the feather duster. I gave her your address."

"Well, if it's her, don't wait for my call!"

"Later, Corky."

I hung up the phone and went to see who was there. I figured it was probably my neighbor Eileen, coming to complain about my cat crapping in her garden again. My kitty has a thing for her lettuce and onions.

I opened the door, and to my surprise it wasn't Eileen. It was the county cop!

"Hello, Corky. Can I speak with you for a minute?"

"Sure. What's up?"

"I need to ask you some questions regarding our investigation."

"Didn't we take care of that already?"

"Well, there's been a new development. Can I come in?"

"Sure, make yourself at home."

This cop was a pretty good guy. He stood up for Travis and me, which really pissed Drew off.

"Corky, the medical report on the body came back this morning."

"So I heard."

"You heard?"

"I just got a call from Travis. He said you were at his shop."

"Then you know about the cause of death?"

"Travis said the guy was electrocuted."

"That's correct."

"He told me they found burns on his ass, but I figured he was just making that part up."

"No, he wasn't making it up."

"Travis actually told the truth? That's a first!"

"Corky, since you were the one who originally found the body in the woods, do you happen to remember seeing anything there that might help explain the burn marks?"

"Officer, why don't we pull up a couple of chairs? I remember stuff better when I'm sitting down."

"I've never heard that before."

"Can I call you by your name?"

"Certainly."

"Well, you need to tell me what it is."

"Officer Nathan Auger."

"Auger? You're not related to the guy who invented the auger brace are you?"

"Not that I'm aware of. What is an auger brace?"

"It's a big old hand drill from years gone by. You don't see them used much anymore, since electric drills took over."

"Interesting. I'll have to pay more attention when I'm at the hardware store."

"I don't know if you'll be lucky enough to see one there anymore. Try the library. They have books that show tool stuff all the way back to the stone-age."

"Corky, as I was saying, do you recall anything unusual in the woods where the body was?"

"Just the foul smell."

"Aaron Palmer mentioned that you saw Mr. Torrelli at his house. Is that correct?"

"I saw him and Anita arguing on their deck when I was working on the barn."

"Did you ever meet Torrelli?"

"Not when he was alive!"

"And you didn't see anything in the woods that might help explain the burn marks?"

"Nope. Just a bunch of blackberries."

"Well, then I guess that's it for now. If you think of anything that might be of interest, would you call me? Here's my card."

"Nate, can I ask you something?"

"Sure, go ahead."

"Were there burns anywhere else on his body, besides his butt?"

"Apparently not. The report only mentions burn marks in the shape of a big circle on his rump."

"Maybe he went bareback riding with Anita?"

"Corky, I don't think that would explain it."

"When Travis told me Torrelli had been electrocuted, I figured he'd pissed on the electric fence. I've heard that a guy can get killed doing that."

"I've heard that story, too. But I've never actually seen a case of it."

"Nate, Travis told me a story one time about

guys getting electrocuted in a tavern."

"I've heard about singers getting shocked by their microphones."

"No, it wasn't that. He said the men's room had one of those long urinal troughs, and there were little metal bugs mounted to it that were wired. If a guy could piss on a bug and still be able to walk, he was considered macho."

"That's certainly one I've never heard before!"

"He said the guys all made a contest out of it, and at the end of the night, the ladies would draw straws for who got to take the winner home."

"Your friend Travis spins a pretty good tale, Corky."

"He's always told me that he gets pretty good tail. I don't know anything about the spinning part."

"Corky, once again, if anything comes to mind that you think might be relevant to the case, please give me a call."

"Okay, Nate. Will do."

"And Corky, it's Nathan, not Nate."

"Sorry."

As I stood at my front door watching Nathan back out of my driveway, I started wondering about Nicky Torrelli. How did a guy from Chicago, wind up here in the middle of nowhere, dead, with a burned ass?

Chapter Thirty-Three

As soon as Officer Nate was out of sight, I reached for the phone and called Travis back.

"Barbershop, this is the hair artist."

"Has anybody ever told you how full of BS you are?"

"Only you, Corky."

"Travis, you didn't tell me you were sending the cop over to visit."

"The cop? You mean it wasn't the feather duster chick at the door?"

"No, it was Officer Nate."

"Well, I didn't send him."

"So, how'd he know where to find me, then?"

"The cops know all sorts of things, Corky. They've always been able to find me when I least expected them."

"Well, that's a whole different subject. I've heard that most police stations have an autographed picture of you hanging on the wall."

"Yeah, it's a bitch being famous, except for the women it's gotten me."

"There you go, spewing more heated air."

"Corky, a customer just walked in. Why don't you come by here so we can discuss the latest development in the case."

"Okay, I'll see you in a bit."

I hung up the phone, and a familiar smell reminded me I needed to empty the cat's litter box again. I wish she would lay off the produce. I hoped Officer Nate didn't get too grossed out.

When I finally got to the barbershop, Travis was busy sharpening his straight razor. He must have just finished up with his customer, cause there was still hair on the floor. He never leaves a mess like that.

"So, Corky, did the cop tell you anything different than what he told me?"

"I don't think so. He wanted to know if I saw anything in the woods that might explain the burn marks."

"Did you?"

"No. I figured Torrelli might have gotten the burns from going bareback riding with Anita. Don't you think it's pretty weird that they're in the shape of a big circle?"

"A big circle? He didn't tell me that."

"Travis, since when do you care what a guy's butt looks like? It's the women's that get your attention."

"Corky, are you sure that's what the cop said?"

"Sure, I'm sure."

"Corky, let me ask you something. How do you think Torrelli got electrocuted?"

"I don't know. Maybe you caught him in bed with your girlfriend?"

"Would you be serious, for once? This information about him being electrocuted, and there being a big round burn mark on his ass, is starting to make sense."

"Maybe to you."

"It reminds me of when I used to hotwire cars. Most of the time it went okay, but every once in a while I'd cross some wires, and sparks would fly."

"I thought you only stole a policeman's motorcycle? Now I find out that you pick locks and hotwire cars, too?"

"Corky, I'm starting to think your pride and joy in the barn had something to do with Torrelli's death."

"The electric throne? Holy crap, Travis!"

"You told me the toilet was made of metal, and wired in reverse, you said it would have shocked the shit out of whoever sat on it. How long after you discovered the faulty wiring did you find his body in the woods?"

"It was the next day."

"So, why couldn't it have been Torrelli who left you the surprise?"

"Not Anita?"

"Well, Leroy told you the Palmers were gone to Canada. Maybe it wasn't Anita, after all. The lab guys can run a test to see if it's his or not."

"No, they can't. I used it for the burn tests after I got the toilet wired correctly."

"Shit!"

"Sorry, Travis, that's no shit."

"Smart ass."

"But we still don't know who messed with the wiring!"

"One thing's for sure, whoever did it had to know something about electricity."

"You're right. Hooking the thing up like that sure wasn't done by accident."

"Corky, do you remember telling me that Jimmy's dad was an electrician, and that Jimmy worked with him for a while?"

"Yeah. Jimmy said he didn't stick with it, cause his dad was always giving him flack."

"But I'll bet he learned enough to be able to hotwire a toilet like that. I think Officer Nate needs to know about this."

"Travis, do you really think he'd believe that Torrelli was done in by a toilet? We couldn't even get Drew to believe we found a body!"

"Yeah, but Drew is an asshole."

Chapter Thirty-Four

"Travis, are you going to make the call to Officer Nate?"

"Corky, maybe we should go home and pack our bags first. After what Drew said about us, if the county boys don't buy what we're selling, we'll really be the laughing stock around town."

"How about we go on the road playing music, and let the cops figure all this out by themselves?"

"That's tempting. But, you know, if we are right, we'll be the town heroes. The women will be lined up at our doors!"

"What women? This is Palmer Lake!"

Travis took Officer Nate's card from his pocket and dialed the phone.

"Okay, Corky, I left word at headquarters for him to call me back."

Travis and I decided to try and relax by playing a game of checkers, and sat down at the table. We were just getting started, when the phone rang.

"Barbershop, Travis speaking."

"This is Officer Nathan Auger. I just got a radio call from headquarters telling me to contact you."

"Officer, Corky and I were just discussing the new information you gave us regarding the body. We think we have some important details for you."

"An hour ago, neither one of you guys had anything new to add. What's this about?"

"Well, the burn marks on his ass got me to thinking. Can you swing by my shop again?"

"I'm across the street at the Bite Time Café, just finishing my lunch. I can be there in a few minutes."

"Great! See you soon."

Travis hung up the phone and started doing a little jig. He was really excited. He even started sweating and turning red.

"What did Officer Nate say?"

"He'll be right over. He's at the Bite Time."

"Travis, you look like you need to use the head."

"I can hardly wait!"

"You better hurry, then, before you piss your pants!"

"Corky, sometimes you really sour the mood!"

"Well, if you're not going to use it, then I am!"

When I came out of the bathroom, Travis was dancing around the room with his coat rack, and singing! I was about to make a comment about how stupid he looked, when in walked Officer Nate.

"Travis, Corky, I see we're giving dance lessons now. Do they come free with a haircut?"

"Officer, take a seat. Corky and I have some new leads."

"I'm not interested in learning those dance steps, if that's what you mean by new leads."

Travis put the coat rack back in the corner, and we all three sat down.

"So, what have you two come up with that's so important?"

"Well, Nate, it's like this."

"Travis, my name is Nathan."

"Well then, Nathan, listen up. Corky told me that Torrelli's burns were in the shape of a big circle. You didn't mention that when you came to see me earlier."

"So?"

"We think he got those burns from an electric toilet."

"A what?"

"Corky, why don't you clue him in."

"Nathan, when I was working on the Palmers' barn, Anita had me install an electric toilet. It's pretty futuristic."

"I suppose it has flashing lights and a siren."

"I'm serious! It's mounted in the tack room!"

"You're pulling my leg."

"No, I'm not! I even put in a new door, so Anita can make her embarrassing noises and not scare the horses!"

"Corky, didn't you tell me she ordered the toilet from some catalog?"

"That's right, Travis. Her neighbor had one installed in their barn, and that's how Anita got the idea."

"You guys should be on late night TV."

"Nathan, I didn't know until Travis told me, but girls who ride horses have to go a lot."

"I need some fresh air!"

"Just keep your seat, Nathan. Look, we know that Torrelli showed up at the Palmer house, cause Corky saw him there arguing with Anita on the deck. Come to find out, he used to be her boyfriend when she lived in Chicago."

"Now, how do you know that?"

"Corky put the screws to her and she confessed."

"I'm still waiting to hear how the magic toilet figures in."

"We think Torrelli showed up at the Palmer place looking for Anita, and wound up down at the barn."

"Nathan, the morning I arrived to finish the electrical hook-up on the toilet, I discovered that someone had messed with the wiring. The toilet had been hotwired, so to speak, and I found an incredibly huge pile under the lid that didn't get incinerated."

"Corky, is this another one of your imaginary stories, like the one about the electrified bugs in the urinal?"

"You told him about that?"

"Travis, we were talking about guys getting electrocuted by pissing on electric fences. I guess I should have told Officer Nathan that after peeing on one of those bugs, you've been able to sing a whole octave higher."

"Officer, Corky and I found out that Leroy Lacome has a cousin named Jimmy Wiseman. Jimmy's girlfriend, Mary Ellen, told us that he wanted to help rid Palmer Lake of the Torrrelli problem."

"The Torrelli problem? You want to explain that?"

"Let's just say that Torrelli wasn't welcome around here."

"So how does this Jimmy Wiseman person figure in?"

"Mary Ellen hooked Jimmy up with the security guard at Palmer Industries, because Torrelli kept showing up there causing trouble."

"I don't get the connection, Travis."

"We think the guard contacted Jimmy the next time Torrelli showed up, and he high-tailed it out to the plant. From there, he followed Torrelli to the Palmers' house."

"You're still not making any sense."

"Jimmy knew he could park next door at the Lacomes' place, and Torrelli wouldn't spot him. From there, he saw Torrelli go to the Palmers' front door, looking for Anita. Torrelli didn't know she was gone to Canada."

"Travis is right, Nathan. Anita went to Canada with her husband, so she could buy stuff from the vending machines in the hotel."

"Travis, is your friend always like this?"

"Officer, as strange as he might seem, he always tells the truth."

"So, continue with your story."

"Jimmy figured that Torrelli would go looking for Anita at the barn next, so he snuck down there and waited for him. That's when he happened to see the wires hanging out of the breaker box and hotwired the toilet."

"Hotwired the toilet? I can only imagine what the captain will say when he hears that!"

"When Torrelli got to the barn, he didn't find Anita, but he did find the toilet, and decided to answer nature's call."

"And you think that's where he was killed?"

"Travis is right, Nathan. The toilet is made of metal, and when his bare ass touched down, zap!"

"Let me see if I understand this. You two are saying that an electric toilet in the barn got hotwired, and when Torrelli sat on it, his bowels exploded, his ass got burned, and he had heart failure and died? I think I'll refer you guys to the comedy club in Keselburg!"

"Nathan, we don't do comedy. Corky and I play music."

"I'm afraid to ask you how his body wound up in the woods."

"Travis, we never talked about that, did we?"

"Corky, I think Jimmy probably loaded the body into a cart or a wheelbarrow and pushed him there. Torrelli was pretty big, and I doubt if Jimmy could have carried him. But, I imagine the lab boys will be able to figure all this out now, thanks to us."

"I'll just bet you guys have the answer to who buried the body in the planter, too."

"Nathan, that one's easy. Mary Ellen said that Jimmy told her he planted the problem. Corky acted on that as a hunch, and found the body in the bathtub."

"You know, when I tell this story back at headquarters, they'll probably put me on school crossing duty."

"Nathan, how come Corky and I seem to have so much trouble convincing lawmen? If it weren't for our investigating, Torrelli would still be missing!"

"Well, I suppose that part's true. Okay, I'll tell your story to the captain, just the way you guys think it happened. If he believes it, there will certainly be more questions, so don't run away."

"You can find us at Bertha's, seven nights a week."

Travis and I watched Nate leave the barbershop, shaking his head and staring into space. When he went to get in his car, he opened the back door by mistake.

"Corky, I don't think he believed a word we said."

"Travis, who cares? I'm impressed by your detective skills! How did you figure all that stuff out?"

"It was the gunshot."

"What gunshot?"

"Don't you remember? When we went snooping at the lake, Mary Ellen and Jimmy started yelling at us from the front door, and we heard a gunshot!"

"Sure, I remember that!"

"Well, when I pulled Torrelli's body out of the blackberry bushes looking for ID, he still had on his shoulder holster, but there was no gun in it."

"So?"

"I think Jimmy's got Torrelli's gun. He fired the shot!"

"Travis, maybe I better switch from beer to bourbon."

"Corky, I'm planning on spending some of my Torrelli loot tonight at Bertha's. Let me buy you a real man's drink, and we can talk about starting our own private detective agency."

"Travis, are you serious?"

"About the drinking I am!"

Chapter Thirty-Five

Officer Nate may not have believed me about the electric bugs in the men's room, but the county police chief believed our story about Jimmy Wiseman and the electric toilet.

Travis and I got to ride along with the cops out to the Palmer place two different times. The county boys wanted all the details of the hotwiring, plus a guided tour of the wooded area where I originally found the body. For some reason, they kept asking me how I knew the body was in the bathtub?

The lab guys were busy collecting fingerprints, as well as taking soil samples from the woods and the planter. To my surprise, they even removed the electric toilet, and took it with them! If Anita was still around, I can only imagine the conversation she would have had with her invisible friend about that!

They found fingerprints other than mine on

the breaker panel and the toilet wiring, and on a couple of the tools hanging in the barn. They also found those prints on the cart used to haul hay bales. Score one for the barber!

Next door at the Lacomes', the same fingerprints showed up on the bathtub planter, and on one of their shovels. Then they found the prints on Leroy's station wagon, as well.

After nonstop hell-raising by Mama, and as a result of finding the unknown fingerprints, Leroy was released from jail and put on probation.

Based on the information Travis and I gave them about the electric toilet being hotwired, the county cops started looking for Jimmy Wiseman. They went to Diamond Car Rentals, but Jimmy wasn't there. Carrot told them Jimmy hadn't shown up for work the past few days, and he didn't have an address for him, because Jimmy had been living in his car.

The county boys were also interested in talking to Mary Ellen Smythe. When they went looking for her at the mayor's office, they were told she was taking some vacation days. Then they drove to her house on the lake, and found the place vacant. The furniture was still there, but that was because the house was a furnished rental. All of Mary Ellen's personal belongings were gone.

The security guard at Palmer Industries told the police he'd never heard of anyone named Jimmy Wiseman. The young man he had been instructed to contact went by the name of Aubrey. He didn't know his last name. To contact Aubrey, he was told to call the mayor's office and leave a message.

The county police issued a wanted bulletin for Jimmy and Mary Ellen, with a reward for information leading to their capture. I was surprised by their disappearance, but it didn't seem to surprise Travis at all. He had his famous, shit-eating grin in full bloom as we discussed their whereabouts over drinks at Bertha's.

"Corky, did you know that Jimmy was living in his car?"

"He never told me that, but when I saw his car at Mary Ellen's, I did notice it was crammed full of stuff."

"I wonder why he wasn't living at her house?"

"Jimmy told me he wanted to drive long-haul trucks. Maybe he was just practicing the lifestyle by living in his car."

"Can you imagine wanting to live in a truck? A night in my van is one thing, but I wouldn't want to wake up there every morning."

"Jimmy told me he'd been trying to save up the money to go to truck driving school. Then, just recently, I guess Mary Ellen gave him the money."

"Really?"

Travis was starting to turn red. Then I could see sweat on his face.

"Travis, what is it? You're getting all hot and bothered again."

TROUBLE COMES TO PALMER LAKE

"Corky, Mary Ellen doesn't make very much working for Mayor Bartholomew. She's told me more than once, if she could find a better paying job, she would move on. I want to know where she came up with the money for Jimmy."

"Maybe she drained her savings account, in the name of true lust!"

"Something's been bugging me, ever since we figured out that Jimmy knocked off Torrelli."

"Like what?"

"Why would Jimmy kill a guy that he didn't even know?"

"Maybe getting rid of Torrelli was his way of showing Mary Ellen he's a man."

"Corky, I'm betting Jimmy got paid to do it. I don't think the money for the driving school came from Mary Ellen at all. I think it came through her."

"Travis, is that your idea of a toilet joke? You expect me to believe that Mary Ellen craps money?"

"You know what? Ever since you met Anita, your brain has been pickled!"

"So, where do you think the money came from?"

"Think about it. Who wanted to make sure that Torrelli never found Anita?"

"Well, there were several people, according to Mary Ellen. They had meetings about that."

"Corky, I think the money came from M.B."

"Attorney Claymore?"

"Exactly. He was the one who set the whole thing up in the first place, getting Anita, or should I say Sherry, released into Aaron Palmer's custody."

The next day, Officer Nate called and told us that the lab boys had found the barn toilet guilty of murder. We also learned that the coroner had finished with Torrelli's body, and Attorney Claymore had left with the corpse, accompanying it back to Chicago for a proper burial.

Travis was going bonkers with his suspicions that Jimmy was hired for the hit on Torrelli. He tried to talk to Officer Nate about it, telling him that Claymore, Mayor Bartholomew, and Sheriff Ledbetter were all in on it, but Nate told him that until the killer was caught, nothing could be done.

Chapter Thirty-Six

As the weeks passed, there were no sightings of Jimmy or Mary Ellen, and Travis had given up any hope of becoming famous with his theory about who hired the hit on Torrelli.

Things seemed to be getting back to normal in Palmer Lake, though. Travis and I were at Bertha's, talking to her about playing music on Saturday nights, and we got to see her throw the Birdman out. One of his parrots landed on a customer's shoulder and made a mess.

Pinkie and Rosie Buettemeier were trolling again. Apparently they got fed up with Billy Hamrod's all-women parties, after all. I was still kind of interested, but Travis turned out to be right about us being the town heroes, so I decided to wait and see what came of that.

The sheriff had taken on a low profile for a week, after being shut down by the county cops.

But now he's back to being himself, telling visitors from out of town, and anybody else that will listen, how he solved the Torrelli murder.

The mayor had to find himself a new secretary, since Mary Ellen disappeared. He wound up hiring Debra, after learning she got straight A's in the prison bookkeeping class. Apparently that was the only thing she got straight.

The hot gossip around the Bite Time Café is currently all about the Palmers. With Anita being enrolled in the mental ward at the Keselburg Hospital, and Aaron having found a new female golf partner at the Keselburg Country Club, the local residents have been provided with a heap of story telling material. And as if that weren't enough, it turns out that Aaron and Anita were never married!

Travis finally got the oil leak fixed on his motorcycle, then went for a test drive after work and wound up at Charlene's. He's been going out every evening since, for more testing.

Now, I have to try and find the time to stop by the barbershop to see him, since he's not on his favorite stool at Bertha's. We both keep wondering about Jimmy and Mary Ellen, trying to figure out where they went.

After having dealt with Anita, her barn toilet, and finding a dead guy, I felt I deserved something really special. So, I grabbed my Torrelli loot, drove to Keselburg, and spent the whole day shopping at Jumbo's Hardware.

I came home with a whole truckload of neat stuff, including a self-cleaning litter box for my cat. But the one item that really excited me the most was the battery-operated toilet plunger. You turn it on, and a laser beam breaks up the blockage. No more sloshing around the old-fashioned way for me!

Being a handyman, I never know from day to day what kinds of situations I'll run into. Back when I started my business in Palmer Lake, I figured I'd be getting my hands dirty, but I sure never expected to wind up in so much crap!

LaVergne, TN USA
11 February 2011
216158LV00001B/1/P